THE PITCHMEN

THE PITCHMEN

DON JAMES

CUTTING EDGE

ISBN-13: 978-1-970848-09-0

Published by
Cutting Edge Books
PO Box 8212
Calabasas, CA 91372
www.cuttingedgebooks.com

CHAPTER ONE

T HE STATE was on daylight saving time and although it was after nine o'clock on this July evening, there still was daylight when Murch Colton arrived at the outskirts of Douglas City. All the way through the mountains, coming inland from the coast, the heat had been building and now it hung like a breathless pressure over the city.

Automatically Murch slowed his car and adjusted his driving to the four-lane freeway traffic as he neared the center of town. This year the West Coast traffic was heavy. Out-of-state cars were pulling up at motels. Roadweathered license plates from New York, Minnesota, Florida, California and many other states seemed to be more in evidence than ever before.

As he approached a turnoff that would take him away from the freeway and up into the West Hills, and the Murchison T. Colton split-level home, Murch debated a moment and then stayed on the freeway. Five minutes later he pulled into another turnoff that took him into the business section.

The streets were strangely quiet compared to the way they were during the day. Lately the night traffic patterns had shifted to the suburban areas, the sprawling supermarket shopping centers, and the new residential areas that once had been farmland. In the city center a good many stores were vacant now, but the office buildings remained farily well filled, and the larger department stores held their own.

Murch had no trouble finding a parking place at the curb near the office building that housed Colton, Lanham and Simpson, Advertising. He had a building key and let himself in and rang for the night man.

An elevator door finally opened and the night man smiled a greeting. "Evening, Mr. Colton! Vacationing? Mighty fine tan!"

"At the beach, John," Murch said. He stepped into the elevator and they discussed the weather and beach for ten floors. The door opened automatically and Murch walked down a deserted hallway to the double doors that bore the firm's name in neat, black letters. He let himself in. The reception room smelled stale despite the air conditioning.

He strode down a short, door-lined hallway to the last door that opened into a corner room. His name was on the door. It was unlocked and he went into the private office. He sat at his desk and turned on a lamp to dissipate the gathing dusk.

For a few moments he shuffled through a week's accumulation of mail, glanced at some notes from his secretary, and then at the hurriedly scribbled message on a sheet of interoffice note paper.

Murch:
    In case you stop at the office, you'll find the letter from LeLane's in your top drawer. I'm at the McPhersons. Call me there. Hurriedly,

Pete

Murch opened his middle desk drawer and took out a letter typed on rich, heavy bond with a letterhead that said simply: *LeLane's Fashions For Women*, with an address and telephone number carefully placed at the bottom of the page. It was a distinctive letterhead, both in type face and layout. This was the letter that had brought the excited telephone call from Pete that morning—the reason why Murch had cut short his vacation.

He looked at the typed message addressed to the agency:

Gentlemen:

We have decided to make a change in advertising agencies and have selected you as one of five agencies which we shall consider.

Since we are a local firm, we assume that you are acquainted with our operation and products. To aid you further in your presentation—should you care to compete for the business—we shall arrange a briefing session with your personnel within the next week and at our mutual convenience. For these arrangements, please call me personally.

Briefly, we anticipate a budget in the neighborhood of $750,000 for the coming year.

If you are interested, we should like to entertain a presentation from your agency on August 7, in our auditorium at the plant.

We realize that this is short notice, but the break with our present agency came unexpectedly, and we want our new agency to prepare our spring-summer-autumn campaigns for next year. Obviously, time is of the essence.

On the other hand, we feel that the dispatch with which an agency may perform under such pressure may be an excellent test of the agency's abilities.

We desire a rather complete presentation including advertising themes, proposed art treatment, media recommendations, sales promotion ideas, and collateral material.

At our proposed briefing we shall further outline our needs and demands from an agency.

I might add that if you accept our invitation your competition will consist of one other local agency and three national agencies.

We would appreciate an immediate reply, and we sincerely hope that you will enter the competition.

Sincerely,

Walter W. Mickels

Advertising Director

Murch carefully read the letter twice, absorbing the message and trying to evaluate the man who had written it. He laid it flat on the desk and stared at it. Three-quarters of a million dollars in billing! With all its accounts, the agency was billing only a little over a million now. This would almost double that figure. *It would do more than that*—it would probably save Colton, Lanham and Simpson from extinction. If they lost the lumber account—and things pointed that way—they would be in trouble, especially since two smaller accounts also were shaky.

He picked up the letter again and studied it, his gray eyes narrowed in thought. Murch Colton, just turned forty-three, looked very much the type-casting concept of the advertising executive.

His hair was cut close to his scalp this year. His body was lean. He looked fit and tan. Golf and his recent week at the beach had helped to create this appearance. His features had a tendency toward the long, narrow face with a thin, sharp nose, a wide mouth, and slightly sunken cheeks, all of which seemed to impart an appearance of nervous energy and concentration.

His smile was ready and winning. His voice was rich and assertive. He wore good clothing on his six feet of bones, sinew and muscle, and he well knew the value of image-impact. He was careful to look the part of the advertising executive. It was, in fact, one of his assets. It had helped him rise from his first job as a junior account-executive to a part ownership in the agency.

Of course, it had taken more than his appearance—the image that he presented to clients—he also had learned the fundamentals of advertising, and he understood and practiced salesmanship. He had cultivated all the other social graces and sophisticated habits to automatically place him in a status level that allowed him the privileges accorded to top executives, vice-presidents and presidents of the various business and civic activities in the city.

Now he read the letter for the fourth time. He had better call Pete Lanham, and he was a little surprised that Lanham would be at the McPhersons. Usually the members of the agency did not associate much during off hours, and he didn't think that Pete had any great love for Mike McPherson, their highly creative art director. But they were undoubtedly discussing the presentation.

He found the McPherson number and dialed. Lorrie McPherson answered the call, her voice sounding friendly and expectant.

"It's Murch, Lorrie," he said. "How are you?"

"Murch! When did you get back?"

"Just now."

"Did Diana come, too?"

"No. We have the beach apartment for two more weeks. She's staying."

"I suppose you want to talk with Pete. Or shall I tell them you're coming right out?"

She made it sound like an invitation, and Murch pictured her at the other end of the wire, visualizing her thin, beautiful body that she liked to clothe in shorts or tightfitting Capris, or peasant dirndl skirts with casual sweaters or shirts.

She still worked at her art on occasion, and sometimes she taught classes at the night community school. She was beautiful enough to pose as a model for any of the classes, but far too talented to waste her time at it.

Murch wondered why she had married Mike McPherson. So did a good many others. Mike had a problem, and a lovely, desirable woman in her early thirties was no answer to it. And he probably created a problem for her.

"I'll be out," Murch said.

"I'll put some Scotch on ice for you right now!"

"Are they talking business?"

"Of course! The LeLane's pitch. They're terribly excited. Aren't you?"

"Yes. We need the account. What about Harold?" Harold Simpson, the third stockholding member of the firm, and the production manager, recently had been hospitalized with his second minor heart attack.

"Fine," Lorrie said. "But they haven't told him. He's not supposed to be excited. And Bill Rhodes is still on vacation. Pete called him. He's coming back by plane—from New York, I think."

"Is Charlotte at your place with Pete?"

"No. She's home with their kids and summer complaint. All of them, Pete says. Poor Charlotte."

"Okay, Lorrie. I'm on my way."

He put down the telephone and thought a moment about Lorrie. As usual, he found himself comparing her with Diana.

Diana, at thirty-eight and after fifteen years of marriage to him, still managed to retain an amazing amount of the pert, good looks that first had attracted him to her.

She was completely unlike Lorrie. She was small, quick, exquisitely formed, and undoubtedly desirable in the eyes of most men. She dressed smartly and seldom wore casuals, as Lorrie did.

She usually looked as if she had just come from a beauty parlor, while Lorrie frequently looked as if a beach wind had tossed her through an open doorway in a confusion of laughter and sunlight.

While Diana had black hair—and she took care that the few gray hairs which appeared were quickly tinted dark—Lorrie had tawny hair that was likely to be sun-streaked in the summer, and it had a narrow band of gray that extended back from over her left eye. And if Diana's dark, brown eyes could flash in anger and impatience, Lorrie's green-blue eyes seemed to reflect strange, hidden depths and moodiness or, occasionally, a great secret happiness.

Murch shook his head, impatient with his thoughts. More and more, lately, he had been making this comparison between the two women. Lorrie was the wife of his art director, a man who was disturbingly demonstrating definite tendencies toward homosexuality. The talk about Mike McPherson and a male librarian had not been without a measure of foundation, Murch knew.

He returned the letter to a desk drawer and left the office. The heat of the street was like a blast from an opened oven when he reached it after the air-conditioned office building.

He drove out of the business district to the heights. The McPhersons lived within a mile of his own place, in a house that was long, low and modern, with a view of the valley. The patio was in the back of the house and Murch knew that they would be out there to get the breeze.

He got out of the car and started toward the house. The door opened and Lorrie McPherson came out. She wore shorts and a halter and she looked very brown in the early darkness. She stood by the doorway, casually erect, her smile showing white against her deep tan. Murch saw the fullness of her breasts straining against the halter, and the smooth, delightful symmetry of her hips and legs so effectively displayed by the shorts she wore.

He came to her and held out a glass of liquid.

"Scotch on the rocks," she said.

"Thanks, Lorrie. I need it."

"And this?" she asked, smiling mischievously. She came against him in a smooth movement and her lips somehow met his. He felt her pressing against him, the firmness of her breasts higher against him than Diana's would have been, and her hips somehow fitting snugly against his, as if they belonged there.

It was not a brazen, bold gesture, but a simple, affectionate and frank expression of sincere liking, and delight at seeing him. She had kissed him before, even as McPherson had pecked at Diana in greeting her at a party, or when they met for a night of bridge.

But, almost instantly, he realized that this time it was something more than a friendly gesture. Perhaps the kiss held for just an instant longer to convey a meaning, or a small and restless invitation. Perhaps he imagined it, but he certainly wasn't imagining the instinctive surge of blood into his groin, and one arm went about her and pulled her tight against him.

They stepped apart and looked at one another. He knew then that she had experienced it, too—whatever it was.

"Well!" she finally said. "I mean, *well!*"

"I'll tell you something," he grinned.

"Nice?"

"I think so. You're lovely, beautiful and exciting. I thought you'd like to know."

"Thank you, Murch."

He sampled the drink. "Let's see what they've dreamed up," he said.

"They're still sober, so I guess they're serious about it. Isn't it exciting, Murch? Do you think we'll get it?"

"We have a chance," he told her. "Just a chance. But we'll give it one hell of a try."

They went through a long living room toward doors that opened upon the patio. She walked easily beside him. He noticed again how much taller than Diana she was.

"If there's any way I could help," she said. "I mean … art or something. It's a fashion account and you'll remember that I've done a little of that. Don't hesitate to ask."

He glanced at her, suddenly remembering that she once had done a series of trade-book ads for LeLane's.

"That's a good idea," he said. "You'd better sit in on our sessions."

"I'd love to—that is, if Mike won't mind. Even if he *is* my husband—" She glanced at him and left the meaning in the air. He understood.

"I'll suggest it so he'll think it's his own idea," Murch told her with a smile.

They walked through the open doorway and across the patio where Pete Lanham and his art director-host sat in lawn chairs, talking excitedly. They looked up and greeted Murch. He and Lorrie sat on a chaise lounge, facing the two men.

"How does it look?" Murch asked. "Do we have a chance?"

Pete Lanham carefully placed his glass on the patio floor. He was a short, thin, quick man whose hair was thinning rapidly, whose eyes looked perpetually owl-like behind large, black-rimmed glasses, and who was one of the most competent account executives and advertising men on the Pacific Coast.

At one time he had worked as a time salesman for a radio station. He had served a year as a production man for a small agency and then had managed to acquire a few accounts for himself, which later enabled him to become a member of Colton, Lanham and Simpson.

He was married to a woman as small, thin and quick as he was. They had four children and were constantly in fear that Charlotte was pregnant again. She was deeply religious and refused to use contraceptives.

As Murch looked at Lanham now, he again was conscious of contrasts. This time he compared the small, thin man against the athletic-appearing, large and handsome McPherson. At first glance most men would have tabbed McPherson as an ex-football player, possibly a fast halfback.

On second glance, the more discerning and worldly men usually caught the slightly offbeat gestures, the almost lilting lift of head, the unmasculine movement of hand and expression of eyes.

Of recent years all these things had become more pronounced, and when McPherson was deep in creative work there occasionally might be a quick, petulant outburst of anger, or a piquancy of displeasure, or a toss of head and nastiness of expression that betrayed the man for what he might be.

Pete and Murch had discussed it one night over too many drinks. Pete had said: "Murch, let's face it. He's a homo. It's been there a long time. I never told you, but he and I went to the U at the same time. There was a deal there. He got mixed up with a male prof. Something happened. We never found out what. Something about a couple of profs finding them together in the profs apartment. Anyhow, the prof resigned and that was when Mike went to art school."

Pete had finished his drink and put the glass down. He had blinked at Murch. "Never knew why he married Lorrie. Never figured that out. Maybe he wanted to make a last try at being normal. But I don't think it worked."

Murch had nodded owlishly, steeped in alcoholic wisdom and understanding. "Some are bisexual," he suggested.

"Could be. But you know what?"

"What, Pete?"

"He's one hell of an art director! I'm glad we've got him."

"Hell, yes! And we keep him," Murch had said. "But never a word to Simpson. Harold wouldn't understand."

Neither Murch nor Pete had discussed the probability of McPherson's homosexuality again. Tonight Murch thought of it as he faced the two men because there was a definite tinge of it in Mike McPherson's great excitement.

"Tell him, Pete! *Tell* him!" Mike implored.

"We've worked up an idea for the presentation," Pete said. "One *hell* of an idea! Mike really came up with it and we need Bill for copy."

Murch smiled and looked at Lorrie. "You didn't tell me," he accused.

She shook her head. "I didn't know. I was watching for you. It must have just happened."

"It did!" McPherson announced. "Right after you left to fix a drink for Murch." He looked at Murch, his eyes gleaming with excitement. "It's terrific, Murch!"

"I'm waiting," Murch said.

"Tell him," McPherson implored again of Pete.

Pete blinked behind the black-rimmed glasses. "It's really something, Murch. Let me give it to you fast. Try it on for size. See how it fits."

Rapidly he sketched out a tentative idea. They would leave the usual presentation format and would create small, intimate, semitheatrical sets, create music if necessary, and pitch the account as it had never been pitched before.

As he talked, Pete's own excitement came into his voice, and McPherson interrupted frequently for quick explanations of art concepts, his graceful hands outlining and delineating, his voice almost lyrical in his enthusiasm.

Murch recognized and sympathized with this exuberance of creative persons. Pete was a creative man, in his own way. As Murch often told clients, "He's the best idea man in the West." McPherson was the essence of the creative man. And he, Murch, had a good share of it, too.

"Slow down," he finally said. "Let's really look at it."

"Well, what do you think?" they asked simultaneously.

"You really may have one hell of an idea. It's different and—"

"That's just the point!" McPherson interrupted triumphantly. "Because it is *different* as a *presentation*, it also shows the client that the *agency* is different—original—creative!"

Murch looked at Lorrie and, from the excitement in her eyes, saw that she, too, had been caught up in the men's enthusiasm. What he saw in her expression also convinced him that he must handle this with care.

In the next few days everyone in the agency—and possibly a wife or two—would have to give a tremendous amount to the effort. There must be no cold water thrown, no discouragement. Everything from now on had to be on the upbeat—but it also had to be carefully right and logically effective.

He finished his drink and lit a cigarette, remembering that he had intended to stop smoking after reading the latest scare about the cancer thing. Well, it would have to wait awhile now. He would need every crutch to help him through the days before him.

"I like it," he said simply. "It's great. When Bill gets here we'll have a think session and round out the whole thing. Meanwhile, let's keep throwing in other ideas. But first of all—" He paused as if a sudden thought had come to him. "First of all, we'd better take them up on their briefing offer. Maybe we'd better check them out before we plan too much. We'd better learn what they really want—their problems—where T. T. I. & Associates let them down. When a national agency like that falls flat on its face, there must be something really wrong somewhere."

"It was the art work," McPherson said scathingly. "Terrible."

"Copy was bad, too," Pete said. "Of course, there can be a lot of other things: media selection, the promotions, trade ads, conflicting personalities. It's hard to know."

"I did some trade stuff for them once," Lorrie volunteered. "I liked working with them."

"That's right," McPherson said. "Lorrie *did* do some stuff for them. Year before last. Trade ads, and really good."

Murch grabbed at the opening. He looked thoughtfully at the art director. "Mike, you've got an idea there. Why don't you put Lorrie to work for you on some of this stuff? With her experience in the line, and with your direction, we should be able to come up with something."

Lorrie acted dismayed, as if she had spoken out of turn. "I don't know if I *could*—"

"Certainly you could!" her husband said emphatically. "You do fashion stuff beautifully. I'll be much too busy to do the roughs, and we couldn't find anyone better than you."

Lorrie glanced at Murch and then at her husband again.

"Well ... if you really think ..."

"Certainly!" McPherson said, as if the matter were closed. "Now about these theatrical sets we mentioned, Murch. As soon as we get the themes, I'll begin my art concepts and—"

Murch laughed and held up his hands. "Mike—wait! We need copy first. You've started the ball rolling, now let's wait until Bill gets here tomorrow."

Pete nodded. "Murch is right—about the copy and about the briefing with LeLane's. I've already arranged the briefing, Murch. I called Mickels as soon as we got the letter and set the date for day after tomorrow. Wanted to make certain we'd have time to get you and Bill here. Okay?"

Murch looked thoughtfully at the smaller man. "Did you have a good talk with Mickels?"

Pete nodded. "I mean, I established a good contact. I've known Walt a long time. Knew him when he was over at Cowper and Andersons and I was selling time. We're sort of old buddies, in a way."

"That's a break," Murch said. He put out his cigarette and looked up at Pete again. "Did you suggest who might handle the account if we should get it?" he asked.

Pete Lanham looked at him and blinked. He no longer appeared to be an eager young creative man in the throes of creation; nor a man who had drunk enough to be overly exuberant about a plan. He looked like a shrewd, calculating, and very tough small man who knew his way around and had climbed to the top of a small pile by stepping on men larger than himself.

Murch recognized this look and wondered momentarily if he would look that way, too, if he had a wife and four kids to support. Murch had a growing suspicion and he wanted an answer.

"Did you?" he asked again, pleasantly enough.

"Yes," Pete said quietly. "I told him *I* probably would handle the account. Is that all right with you, Murch?"

Murch smiled, feeling his lips become stiff, and trying not to narrow his eyes. He reminded himself that this wasn't the time for dissension. First of all, they had to create the pitch, get the agency to work. Above everything else they had to get the account, or there probably would be no agency in another six months.

Whatever Pete might have thought during the slight delay in Murch's reply, he concealed it well with his smile. "It *is*, isn't it?" he asked again.

"I don't know," Murch said. "We'll discuss it later." He stood up. "How about nine in the morning? Okay?"

"Fine," Pete said and got up. "I have to go home. Charlotte's having a hell of a time with the kids. Summer complaint."

"It's the water," McPherson said petulantly. Lorrie joined the three men as they went toward the house. In the living room she detained Murch.

"Come into the studio, Murch. I want you to see my latest. Pete already has."

"Terrific!" Pete said. "Go look at it, Murch. See you in the morning."

He and McPherson went out of the house and toward the parked cars. Lorrie led Murch to the studio and showed him her painting. It was a portrait of a Negro girl with bared breasts. The picture had a deep, disturbing moodiness. Murch recognized the talent in the work.

"Like it?" Lorrie asked.

"Yes," he said softly. "Very much."

"I'm glad," she said. From outside the house came the voices of the two men as they talked beside Pete's car. Lorrie faced Murch and he was puzzled by the expression in her eyes, and her smile.

"Thanks for dealing me in," she said. "You did it nicely, and I do want to work on the presentation."

"I *want* you to work on it."

"I don't think Pete should be the account man," she said in a calm, direct voice.

Though Murch believed office politics had no place in the homes of the employees, especially with the employees' wives, he knew that to shrug off her statement would be useless, and almost an insult to a direct offer of understanding from a lovely and discerning woman.

He said. "We both know it. Thanks. You're quite a woman, Lorrie. I mean that."

"I *could* be," she said very quietly. "I truly *could* be, Murch."

For the second time that night, and while they heard Pete and Mike talking outside, she came close to him, looked up with her disturbing, steady gaze, and offered her lips. He accepted the offer because suddenly he wanted to kiss her more than anything he had wanted in a long time. This time he strained her to him, an he made no comparisons with Diana. When they stood apart again, she took a deep, tremulous breath.

"I wouldn't do that if I weren't certain," she said.

"About what?" he asked.

"That you and Diana aren't—" She vainly sought a word, and then shrugged a little. "I guess it's no secret among us—about you and Diana."

"Let's not—" He'd started to rebuke her for mentioning his problems with Diana, and then realized she wasn't offering criticism or ordinary bitchiness. Nor was she offering him sympathy or a cheap affair.

Unless he was greatly mistaken, Lorrie had her own marital problems. If it was true—and he was almost certain that it was—he wondered how a woman who was as obviously warm, healthy and female as Lorrie could live with a man who might have lost almost all his male interest in women.

Murch shook his head. "No," he said. "I mean … it isn't good between Diana and me. Maybe it never was. I've never told anyone. I never wanted to admit it."

"I know," she said. "There are things which I'd rather die than admit."

He knew then that he was right about her. Dimly he was aware of the conversation outside the house, and the sound of their own breathing as they stood close.

He began to reach for her again, and then shook his head and started to draw back his hands. "It'd be like a forest fire," he said. "I don't want to do that to us."

She took his hands, brought them to the halter she wore and held the palms of his hands against her breasts. She pressed them there and she breathed quickly and said, "Now do you know?"

"Yes," he said, aware of sudden, intense desire for her.

She slowly released his hands and said, "It's time you should know. We're not getting any younger, and the two situations aren't getting any better. Maybe it's time—"

She turned abruptly and walked out of the study. He followed her, watching the firm, feminine rise and fall of her buttocks, the swing of her hips and legs, and suddenly wanting her as he had wanted no woman since the early confused days of his budding adolescence and onslaught of sexual awareness.

"Soon?" he asked softly.

"Soon," she said over a shoulder, without turning her face, but confirming her promise with a quick nod.

They went out to the driveway where Pete had just started his car. "Isn't she terrific?" he called to Murch.

"Terrific," Murch replied.

"You ever want to sell that black gal, you let me know, Lorrie!" Pete said, taking on a Southern accent. "You hear?"

"I hear," she smiled. "But she's not for sale. She's too much a part of me, and I never sell *any* of me."

Peter grinned and, with a wave, drove off.

"I never sell any of me," Lorrie said again, softly so that only Murch could hear her. "I only give …"

CHAPTER TWO

MURCH DROVE HOME SLOWLY, remembering the evening, and especially what had happened between Lorrie and him. He told himself he should be centering his full attention upon the forthcoming presentation. But at the moment the LeLane's pitch, the state of the agency, the problem he knew he was going to have with Pete, were all secondary. Lorrie occupied his mind.

Suddenly he realized he was not surprised by what had happened between them. There had been many times when he had looked at her with a carefully concealed desire.

He supposed that all men probably looked at a great many women, wondering how they would be in bed, what they would be like in intimacy. Certainly history, fiction, and newspaper headlines were ample proof that the thought often gave birth to the deed! And he was no exception.

He had been as guilty as others of viewing a girl's bust, her buttocks, legs, thighs, lips, eyes, hair and hands with a vagrant but contemplative thought about her availability and sexual potentialities. "Standing on the corner, watching all the girls go by," was an international avocation of men, and had been almost since time began, he supposed.

With Lorrie it had been different for him. Not only had he been sexually conscious of her, and wondered about her, but not infrequently he had wondered how marriage would be with her. He had carried the fantasies beyond the bedroom to the daily routine of living together.

Leaving sex out of it, Diana and I are not compatible, he thought. *Lorrie and I probably would be.* He stopped the car at a red blinker, and started again, turning into a through street. *Leaving sex* in *it, Lorrie might be even more exciting! And certainly we both have the capacity for love.*

He fumbled for a cigarette and lit it. Suddenly he realized that it no longer was a guessing game, or a secret fantasy, or something to think about without believing it could ever happen.

Murch thought back to the few times he had strayed from his marriage bed—once with a call girl when he was drunk in New York on a business trip; and once with the wife of a client. Both instances had happened more than five years before. Lately there had been no opportunities, and no great desire to create them.

However, there *had* been a growing interest in Lorrie McPherson—the looking at her, liking to talk with her, thinking about her, and the building of a close friendship. And tonight Lorrie had made it plain. She was available. Not because she wanted just to have an affair, he knew, but because she wanted *him*.

The thought almost frightened him. To wish for something while telling yourself that you could never have it, was one thing; to wish for something and abruptly realize you *could* have it, was something else!

The two infidelities he had experienced had been almost accidental, and certainly unplanned: the call girl while he was drunk; the client's wife after a drinking party at a country club— a fumbled, hurried contact on the back seat of a parked automobile; something that now made him uncomfortably ashamed. There had been more dignity with the call girl. At least they had gone to bed.

But an affair with Lorrie would be a major step in his life. Instinctively he knew that it would not be a one-time thing. It would be time and time again, with secret meetings and all the small subterfuges, deceptions and safeguards that would have to be set up. Too, there would be the changed feeling toward Diana. And what about Mike McPherson? Of course, there could be divorce—

The LeLane's presentation came to his mind again as he turned into his driveway. He had to do some thinking about that. As acknowledged head, and president, of the agency, the responsibility was basically his.

They needed the account desperately. Sixteen employees depended upon the agency for livelihoods. To some, the agency meant only a job that could be transferred elsewhere within a few days if anything happened. To others—the stockholders and the principals (a favorite word among agencies)—careers were at stake. Life savings were involved. Homes could be lost, security gone.

He was the only one in the agency who knew how precarious the situation was because the three doubtful accounts were his responsibility.

Douglas Lumber Mills, Inc., had been caught in the lumber depression and was being pressed by a larger competitor to sell out. Murch sensed that the Douglas people were running scared and might very well sell. They billed close to $300,000. Two other accounts, although smaller, were just as shaky.

He had mentioned nothing about the situation to anyone at the agency. There was nothing to be done. It was not a question of losing accounts to other agencies, or a failure to do a good job. It was a situation where one account—the largest—would cease to exist if it sold out. The two other accounts were in financial trouble and no amount of advertising would help. They had over-expanded in a seller's market and now suffered as the buyers took over.

Pete senses it, he thought. *He knows we're in trouble—that I am. If we land LeLane's and he deals himself in as top man on the account, that puts him in the driver's seat if I lose the others. He could even pull out, form his own agency, and leave Harold and me holding the bag.*

He left his car in his driveway and let himself into the house.

They had ordered newspapers stopped for the vacation absence, but there was an accumulation of mail in the inside box. He glanced through it rapidly, saw nothing of importance, and went into the living room, snapping on lights. The place smelled hot and stale. He opened several windows and a faint breeze stirred through the screens.

In the kitchen he mixed a stiff drink and then went to the master bedroom and undressed. He took a shower and finished the drink, sitting naked on the side of his twin bed, gazing thoughtfully across the room in the soft glow of a bed lamp.

Pete's call to Mickels bothered him.

That little son-of-a-bitch is setting this up for himself, he thought. *He's got Mike steamed up his way. I'll have to watch this. I'll grab Bill as soon as he gets in. He'll see it my way. I think he suspects that we're shaky with Douglas and those other accounts. He's smart and he's in a spot to know. I'll talk with him about it. He keeps a close mouth.*

He finished his drink, found fresh pajamas and put them on. He went through the house, turned out lights, and returned to the bedroom. It still was hot. He stretched out and sipped his drink in the darkness of the room. He wasn't sleepy. He began to think about Lorrie again.

At that moment, 2,000 miles across the continent, and some 12,000 feet in the air, Bill Rhodes sat in a jet plane and thought about the Madison Avenue office he had visited three days before.

There might have been a job there. His long-time friend, who now was a vice president of the huge agency, had suggested it. And for a few moments Bill had played with the idea before dismissing it.

He was afraid of the "difference." He always called it that. What he really meant was that he feared the increased pace of the larger, international agency; the power politics; the constant problem of image maintenance; the trauma.

That was a good word for it, trauma—the injury, the wound. If you wanted to stay there you were certain to get it sooner or later; the psychic wound, the physical hurt, the thing that could make you into what some of the others were: defensive and ruthless. It was easier to handle things in a small agency—on the West Coast, and to hell with the big salaries and bonuses and the trauma.

Besides, Kate was in New York—Kate Rhodes because she had kept his name after the divorce five years ago. She had disliked her maiden name. So Kate Rhodes was a name in TV, in advertising circles, on Madison Avenue, in the big agency where she was director of the television and radio department and of two important accounts.

She was smart, competent, and still beautiful. She was the Fifth Avenue, Sunset at Vine concept of outstanding career woman. She was 34, 10 years Bill's junior. They had been married only three years when she had left him for no one else other than herself and her driving ambition. If she needed men in her life, it was to use them and have them on demand, but not as permanent fixtures.

The trouble was—he still loved her. He had taken her to lunch and it had been friendly and very sophisticated. For the first time, however, he noticed the small wrinkles at the corners of her eyes, and the slightly case-hardened smartness of what once had been fresh and youthful beauty. She still made men turn their heads, and women looked her up and down in appreciative appraisal, but she was different.

No matter, he realized. He still loved her and it had been a mistake to spend his vacation in New York; to see her again. He actually was happy when Pete's call had come and he had learned about the invitation to pitch the LeLane's account. At least he could leave New York without feeling that he was running away. He was glad to be headed back toward Douglas City.

As a matter of fact, he thought, he would also be glad to see Linda Smith again. After smart, sophisticated, brittle Kate—who had been his wife once, who had slept with him years ago, and who had responded to his marital lovemaking—it would be a relief to see the eager, starry-eyed freshness of the girl copywriter he had hired five months ago.

Linda had said, "Mr. Rhodes, I know I'm inexperienced, that I'm just out of school, and probably walking around with stars in my eyes, but I want to be a copywriter. I want to be in advertising. I want to learn all there is to know about it! I'll work hard and I'll listen and learn and write my head off!"

He had looked at her in his small office, seeing that there really were stars in her light blue eyes, and knowing she spoke the truth about what she wanted and what she would do. She was pretty—blond and neatly built. She was almost beautiful, except that she still was too young to generate the full excitement of mature womanhood.

They had needed someone to write TV scripts and retail copy for small accounts. The job didn't pay much, but that didn't matter to her. He hired her and she began to work her heart out for the agency, and for him.

He smiled at the thought of her and rested his head back and looked down the aisle at the stewardess who walked toward him.

Idly, he wondered if the stewardess would see him for what he was: a too thin, too tired, sandy-haired man of 44; a good copywriter; a well-read and fairly talented man who had a way with words, possibly a slight deficiency in ambition, a gift of empathy and sympathy for others, and a flair for bachelorhood simply because he still loved Kate, the woman who had left him and divorced him.

"The bitch!" he said softly to himself, and smiled. *Kate—the aphrodisiacal, talented, competent, heartless bitch. I still wanted to take her to bed.*

He shook his head in self-amusement and lit a cigarette. The stewardess smiled at him as she passed. He looked out the window and saw lights far below and wondered what city they were over.

If he couldn't sleep, maybe he could get some ideas about a pitch for LeLane's. The agency needed the account—more than anyone except Murch realized. Or maybe Pete did know and was going to try a power play; grab the LeLane's account for himself and then set up his own agency, cutting Murch out. It could happen. Especially if Murch lost Douglas Lumber.

He wondered if Pete did know about Douglas Lumber. He thought not. Murch had kept the situation well concealed. But he—Bill—had his own pipeline into Douglas Lumber. A copy chief frequently maintains his own contact in a client's organization. And Bill's contact had most confidentially admitted that it looked as if Douglas Lumber was about to be sold.

This whole thing could blow, he thought. *And I don't trust Pete. He's a hard, tough, ruthless little bastard."*

He put out his cigarette and closed his eyes to think about the LeLane's pitch; surprisingly, he went to sleep. He was right about himself. He was too thin and too tired.

The night was cool at the coast and the breakers seemed very white as they curled along the beach below the modern, expensive apartment resort where Diana Colton sat at a window and slowly sipped a gin and tonic. Lately she had taken to gin and tonic as a most satisfactory drink. In town she frequently tried tonic and vodka or she made vodka gimlets, because the vodka was not so noticeable upon her breath—if at all.

When a woman is thirty-eight and begins to drink because she is bored, or a little afraid that forty is coming much too quickly, or because each morning the small lines and slight sagging of skin are uncomforting warnings, it may be easy to drink a little too much and too frequently.

Diana sometimes thought that thirty-eight was a bad age. A good many things could bother a woman at that age. Her husband could. Their marriage relationship could. This evening Diana had summed it up very neatly in her own thoughts as she sat alone and watched the restless surge of the Pacific.

"I want him. I'm hungry for him. I'm jealous of him. But I don't really love him. I want a man and I have a man—but so much of our marriage has become a bore. Or is *mundane* the word?"

Since she could remember, Diana had set her sights upon what she wanted, and then she had directed her quick, nervous energy toward attaining her goals selfishly and frequently callously.

She had decided upon marriage in the same way. She had selected Murch Colton, gone after him, and landed him. Not that there was anything unpleasant about it. She had liked him enough to marry him; he was attractive; he aroused her sexually; he had a good background, money-earning ability, and probably a future. They were of the same religion, and they had a great many friends and interests in common. So she had decided to have him for a husband and, once she had decided, she set about getting him with determination and no little skill.

Despite her decision, there had been one slight flaw in all of it. Even as she set her cap for Murch and began the campaign, she still was in love with a boy named Sean O'Brien.

This had happened during her last year at college. O'Brien had been a handsome, wild, irresponsible, hard-drinking, and wholly attractive youth who had done what no one else had ever managed to do before—or since. He had made Diana lose her head about someone other than herself.

Diana had lost more than her cold logic and common sense over him. One night, on the back seat of his battered car, she had willingly sacrificed her virginity to him.

That probably had been her mistake. Once he had won the game, Sean O'Brien soon had dropped her for a fresh-from-a-cattle-ranch coed with red hair and freckles around her nose. He had been equally successful but less fortunate with the red-headed coed. She became pregnant and within a few months she was Mrs. Sean O'Brien and the couple was living on the home ranch in eastern Oregon within a year.

Diana never was to forget Sean O'Brien—for the love she had held for him, for the touch of inane romance he had brought her, and for the stark fact that Sean O'Brien had taken her virginity.

She never told Murch, and she had managed enough hesitance and physical reaction on her first night with him to convince him that she had been as virginal as she had pretended to be.

Her sexual life with Murch had been satisfactory. It never had reached the heights she had known with Sean, but it had become a competent and wholly pleasant experience, to be mutually shared whenever they desired.

Sitting at the picture window, shielded from the outside beach chill, Diana sipped again at her drink and occasionally puffed at a cigarette. Murch had left in midafternoon after Pete Lanham had called concerning the chance to make a presentation to the LeLane's people.

She could understand the importance of the account, and the necessity of his returning in the middle of their vacation, but she was worried about something else.

"I must go in," he had told her. "We need the account. I'm sorry, Diana."

"I understand. How soon are you leaving?"

He had just returned from the beach, showered, and had draped a towel around his middle to come out and take the telephone call. She had looked at his tanned body, his obvious male strength and vigor, and suddenly she had wanted him. It was one of the strange and compelling impulses that occasionally came over her; a selfish impulse born of a selfish need to satisfy her own desires.

Confidently she had crossed the room to press against him with a quick and warm kiss in an obvious gesture.

"You have time, haven't you?" she had cooed, brazenly making her availability known to him.

He had looked at her, almost puzzled, and then he had smiled ruefully. "It'll have to wait, I guess. I want to get to the office. I don't quite trust Pete. If you and I start fooling around now—well, you know how it goes …"

For a second she thought he was joking, and then she caught the look of decision in his eyes and, for the first time since she could remember, she had been repulsed. Her offer of sexual availability had been refused.

She'd blushed with a quick anger and she had started to lash out at him with a senseless remark, but had stopped herself. A new thought came, almost like a chill: *Have I ceased to be attractive?* Was she becoming jaded or worn or old or undesirable? She couldn't be!

A woman in her thirties was supposed to be at the height of her natural loveliness. This was the time she had so much to offer, could be so exciting, could satisfy so expertly! Surely Murch knew that. Only two nights before he had given every evidence of knowing it! But now he appeared to be completely uninterested.

She had forced a smile and said, "It probably isn't a very good idea. You *should* get there as soon as you can, darling."

And it had ended there. Only the hurt and anger had remained, and gradually the worrisome doubts came alive again: Was she losing the things that made her attractive to men? Was some of the odd incompatibility between her and Murch due to a lack of interest upon his part rather than the product of boredom?

She finished her drink and went into the bedroom to change into stretch Capris and a sweater. In the well-lighted bathroom she carefully inspected her face.

"I'm still pretty," she assured herself. "I'm still attractive."

She left the apartment and went to the resort lounge, with its game tables and small, cozy bar. She looked around the room and saw Rick Andes standing at the bar.

She liked to look at him. She remembered seeing him play professional football once—a large, dominant, relentless fullback who had virtually won the game single-handed with his powerful drives.

In football gear he had appeared to be huge. Standing at the bar in slacks and a slipover sweater, he looked slimmer and taller, but just as powerful. He was muscle-rippled, brown, and completely masculine. His tanned hands fascinated her with their obvious strength. She could almost feel them. When he raised his drink, arm muscles moved in a symmetrical pattern. She wondered how his arms would feel around a woman.

She had watched him on the beach, sunning, walking, passing a football with some high-school kids who obviously idolized him. She had watched girls try to attract his attention, listened to their remarks about him, and their excited comments when he had spent a day on the beach with a girl who had appeared mysteriously in a California sports car and had disappeared as mysteriously that evening, while Rick resumed his lone drinking at the bar.

Then Diana had met him. Murch knew him and had invited him to their table for a drink. Andes was on vacation from his daily TV interview show on a Douglas City station. He did the show exceedingly well for an ex-pro football player. He was ruggedly handsome, with dark brown eyes, close-cropped black hair, and a relaxed ease on camera. He was popular with both sexes.

The drinks together became a nightly ritual, and Diana felt a thrill of anticipation as she looked at Rick Andes from the doorway. Tonight would be different. There would be just the two of them. She went to the bar and slid onto the stool beside him.

"Buy a deserted woman a drink?" she asked.

His smile was very white against his tanned skin. "What happened to Murch?"

"He had to go in. A sudden business deal. I'll probably be here alone for another week or more."

He nodded, as if there was nothing unusual about Murch's sudden return to the city. "Ad men," he said. "Almost as bad as TV. Gin and tonic?"

"Lovely."

He ordered the drink and for a few moments they lapsed into inconsequential conversation.

"I really don't need this," Diana said as she took the drink. "I've been a lone drinker ever since dinner."

"I've had a few myself," Andes admitted. "I'll make a deal. There's a foreign film playing down at the village. Think Murch would object if we went?"

"He'd be delighted," she assured him. "Ad men are very broad-minded about wives, you know." They laughed and finished their drinks before going out to his car.

The show was just starting and they sat in the small theater, watching the Italian scenery and dramatics, the love scenes, while dubbed-in voices made English come from lips that spoke Italian.

Occasionally their bare arms touched and Diana was very conscious of his presence beside her, the warmness of his skin, the breadth of him and the heavy outline of sinewy thighs under the slacks.

She thought about Murch and made her comparison, even as in a distant city Murch had made a comparison concerning her. Murch was a man. There was no doubt about that. But Rick Andes was not only completely a man, but he was also excitingly, fundamentally male, and he was insidiously arousing the female in her by only sitting beside her and being there so that she was conscious of his body with all its intense strength and drive.

She shuddered a little and caught at her lip. Not since Sean O'Brien had she felt quite like this, and it frightened her. Rick glanced at her face.

"Chilly?" he asked. He had noticed the shudder.

"No—just a delinquent shudder," she smiled.

"Reflex." He nodded and resumed watching the show. But for an instant one of his large hands closed over one of hers. He freed it almost instantly, but there had been a quick communion between them.

Actually it was an excellent movie and they enjoyed it. The theme had been unconventional, the acting superb, and some of the scenes would not have passed a good many censor boards.

On the way back they talked about it. He parked in the common parking area and they walked to her apartment. The resort was quiet; most apartments were dark. It was after midnight.

"Nightcap?" she asked at her door.

He seemed to hesitate.

"Please do," she urged. "I feel talkative."

"It's an idea," he said.

They went into the apartment. It was high on a bluff so that there was no need to pull drapes for privacy. The ocean spread before them in the night, and from the beach came the endless roar of surf.

"It's chilly," she said. "If you'll build a fire in the fireplace, I'll get the drinks. Bourbon?"

"Fine."

Later, they sat on a large divan before the fireplace with lights turned out so only the glow of the fire was in the room and the picture window held the blackness of the ocean and distant stars.

"Tell me about yourself," Diana said. "I mean more."

"More about what?" he asked.

"More than I know: that you were a football star, that you have a successful TV show, that you aren't married, and that you had all the girls agog with your visitor in the sports car."

He smiled. "She's from San Francisco."

"That's all?"

"That's all. Just a nice girl. Anything else?"

"Where were you born? Things like that—"

"Easy. Born in Lead, South Dakota, where my Old Man worked in the Homestake Mine. I grew up in mining camps and finally went to Montana School of Mines in Butte. Played pretty fair football, and after a couple of years I gave up mining for the gridiron. When a bad knee and a few too many years knocked me out of that, I landed in television and Douglas City. End of story."

"Not at all, Rick! The television part?"

He sampled his drink before replying. "Not really unusual. I did sportcasts for a while after I quit playing. One thing led to another—not a network, but at least to the station in Douglas City and my own show, such as it is. I still do sports occasionally. Some go network."

"And never married?"

"Once," he said. He got up and fixed fresh drinks for them. "It didn't work."

"Your show is good. I watch it. You have a way of interviewing. People like you."

"Luck," he said with a grin. "And thirty-eight years of seasoning."

"You're thirty-eight?"

"You sound like that's special—or bad."

"That's *my* age."

"A good year, I think. You wear it well."

"You don't talk like a football pro—at least, I don't think you do."

"I'm not. I'm a TV showman now. There's a difference."

"Not the way I saw you passing a football on the beach."

"Those kids are great." He put his glass on the floor and lit cigarettes for them. "That girl in the show tonight. She was something, too."

"Sex?"

"Maybe. I don't know. A woman has it or she doesn't. You do."

She looked at him, slightly surprised yet greatly pleased. She needed to bolster her opinion of herself; to heal the rebuff she felt she had suffered from Murch. She wanted another man to tell her she was attractive.

"Don't stop!" she smiled. "Anything more?"

He picked up his drink and looked at her. She downed her own, returning his gaze over the rim of her glass.

"Quite a bit more," he said. "You're attractive. You're more than pretty. You're well built—well put together and coordinated. I'm conscious of bodies. Athlete-conscious, I suppose. You walk well and you relax well."

"Relaxing is important in sports, isn't it?"

"It's everything. Tighten up and you're in trouble."

"About one more drink and I'll be *very* relaxed," she said. "But I'll have it if you'll fix it."

"Good." He got up and fixed the drinks. She watched him, seeing the flat breadth of his shoulders, the strong legs and thighs, and again the ripple of arm muscles as he busied himself.

Then she deliberately stood and went to the window, knowing that the faint outside light of night outlined her Capris-clad legs and thighs in almost naked relief, and feeling his eyes upon her as he came toward her with the drinks.

He stood behind her, so close that she could almost feel the heat from his body, handing her the drink with an arm circling around her in movement.

Abruptly, desire came over her in a warm, tremulous wave so that it made her catch her breath, and almost shamefully she felt the readiness of her body. She didn't move. She didn't dare.

Behind her it seemed that his breathing had quickened. Then she felt him against her. She leaned back to him. The drinks were strongly felt now. Inhibitions were fading into the night so that only the glow of the fire, the concealed shelter of the apartment, the locked door, and the nearness of the man were important.

Blindly she put down her drink on a table by them. Her hand touched his glass as he set it down. She felt his hands on her shoulders. He turned her so that he looked down into her face.

"Why not?" he said.

He kissed her. It was like being swept into a vortex of sensation. She closed her eyes and clung to him, feeling the strength of arms and the startling, dominating hardness of his body muscles against her. She felt lost and helpless against his broadness and strength. There was nothing to remind her of Murch or of Sean O'Brien. This was a wholly new experience and she was completely lost and helpless in it, as if she were being ravished and completely subjugated.

She shut her eyes and made no protest, no whispered word of remonstrance, no shake of head, no restraining hand as he carried her past the divan and into the bedroom.

She felt him put her down on a bed and she kept her eyes closed, her arms falling limply at her sides. Only her lips moved as he kissed her, and she surrendered to the deep-kiss union.

His large, strong, capable hands were oddly and gently efficient as they took off her loafers, stripped the Capris from her, pulled the sweater over her head, unfastened and removed her brassiere, and finally lifted her hips to skillfully remove the last garment.

He left her and she kept her eyes closed. Only once did a sensible thought come to her mind, and that was to remember the date and that the probability of her becoming pregnant would be virtually nil. The timing was right.

His weight was heavy on the bed. His lips found her shoulders, her breasts. His gentle, strong hands made silent love to her body. He moved her at will, prepared her for acceptance, and she caught her breath as she felt the deep breadth of his athlete's chest gently cover her breasts, felt the cupped demand of his hands beneath her. Then he had joined with her so that she gasped and clung to him in frantic deliverance.

Later, when he had finished, she was motionless, exhausted, and possessed as she never had been by Sean O'Brien or by Murch. She supposed she should feel shame, remorse, hatred with herself—but she could only lie motionless, her body soft and helpless, her lips bruised, her breasts aching slightly, and a strange and almost eerie peace of saturation flowing over her like a warm caress.

"That was good," Rick said quietly. He was stretched out beside her, on his back, and he had got up to find a cigarette. She had refused one with a shake of her head. She needed nothing now. Nothing at all. She was replete.

The fire of his cigarette glowed as he inhaled. "Good," he said again. "You're good. Do you know that, Diana?"

She smiled, suddenly very glad that he thought her good. She didn't remember much about it, except that she had been frantic and active; crying aloud as she demanded the powerful onslaught of his love-making.

"You're one hell of a woman," Rick said. "Terrific!"

She smiled again. This was exactly what she wanted to hear; to prove to herself that she could be that for a man. At thirty-eight she still could be "one hell of a woman" for a man like Rick Andes.

"I'm glad," she said softly. "Let's sleep awhile. You don't have to go. We haven't finished yet. ..."

CHAPTER THREE

Walter W. Mickels sat at the head of the long table in the conference room at LeLane's administration building. Just turned thirty-five years of age, Mickels had been married and divorced twice. It was not improbable that sooner or later he would be married again. He was attractive to women, and was attracted by them. Men did not especially like him, but he had a capacity to impress his superiors and enough ability to handle his job as advertising director of LeLane's.

Sitting at the head of the conference table was exactly to his liking. This morning he wore a smart, summer-weight worsted suit. He also wore black-rimmed glasses not unlike the ones worn by Pete Lanham, who sat at his right; but unlike Pete he was tall, broad, and as self-assured of his good looks as a movie star coming on the set in the presence of extras.

He also was very self-assured about his task, and about his importance to the advertising people gathered around the table.

He smiled and looked at each visitor separately, as if to grant the visitor permission to be seated at the table. The agency men included Murch, Pete, Bill Rhodes and Mike McPherson. Each had a notebook and pencil. Mickels carefully extinguished his own cigarette and settled back in the chair that usually was occupied by the firm's president.

"All right, gentlemen," he said. "Shall we have at it?"

Murch and Bill exchanged brief glances, their mutual dislike for this man carefully concealed from the others. Pete lit a fresh cigarette and smiled familiarly at their host. Mike McPherson made ready to take notes.

Pete said, "Walt, maybe you'd better start the ball rolling. You know more about this than anyone."

Mickels gave Pete a friendly nod. "I suppose I do," he acknowledged. "And I can spell it out quickly and to the point."

"Exactly why we're here," Pete said.

"First of all, we'll want additional facts about your agency. I want to visit your offices and size you up on your home ground."

"We'll be delighted to have you," Pete said quickly. "Just name the time."

"As for the rest—I'll give you a memo so you needn't take this down—here are a few things we'll want to know in detail: facts about your past experience with accounts; accounts you may have that are allied to ours; the number of employees you have, their backgrounds, and how you would staff up to handle our account. We'd like a résumé of some more important campaigns you've created. Also—how you test, if you do test. Your methods of handling media. Clear?"

"Clear," Pete said alertly. Despite the promise of a memo, he had been taking notes industriously.

Murch looked at Pete. The small, ambitious man was obviously attempting to take control of the situation from the agency side of the table. Taking the notes was a lot of malarkey, Murch thought. Mickels was simply parroting the *How To Select An Advertising Agency* suggestions from any one of a good number of books and articles concerning advertising.

Murch said pleasantly, "We assume you'd like a financial report from us?"

"By all means," Mickels said. "I mentioned that to Pete. He said he'd take care of all that."

"I forgot to tell you, Murch," Pete murmured.

Murch nodded. Pete had started to establish himself early.

Mickels looked around. "And now I think we should have a quick tour through the plant. Afterwards, we'll take a look at the line we're manufacturing. I'll fill you in as we go along. Okay?"

"Excellent!" said Pete.

Again Murch and Bill exchanged glances.

The tour occupied two hours. When they had finished they had seen most of the plant operations and a good deal of the line of garments being produced. They had chatted with designers, production heads, salespeople, and finally with Sam Gortzein, the small, dried-up, elderly president of LeLane's.

Gortzein appraised the advertising man with shrewd eyes, his smile constant, his voice heavy with the accent he had brought out West from New York many years before.

"You are making a presentation, maybe?" he asked.

"We certainly are, Mr. Gortzein!" Pete asserted. "As a matter of fact, we already have some ideas such as you've never seen! And our tour this morning with Walt has been a gold mine of information and inspiration to us."

Gortzein continued to smile, nodding, almost patiently.

"We're ready to compete with any agency," Pete declared.

Murch felt an impatient urge to tell Pete to shut up. He was trying too hard. This dried, bald-headed little man called Gortzein was wise beyond the ages. As a matter of fact, Murch had a brief moment of puzzlement wondering why Gortzein seemed to be so sold on Walter Mickels. Possibly Mickels was clever at selling himself, or more likely Mickels simply jumped at the end of the puppet strings that Gortzein manipulated behind the scenes.

Mickels was playing his part nicely. He was shaking his head and smiling. "I may as well warn you people that I won't do the deciding," he said. "The boss here will do that. And he's forgotten more about this business than most of us will ever learn."

The wizened small man glanced at his employee and smiled again. "A salesman, yet," he said. "So all right. I'll be watching for your pitch. Good luck."

He left them and the small group walked toward the company cafeteria for coffee.

"Great guy," Mickels told them. "A big man in the garment business. Believe me."

"We're impressed with your whole setup," Pete said.

They got coffee and found an empty table.

"Well," Mickels said, "you've about had the whole ball of wax. You've seen the plant, the operation, and the LeLane's line. I've briefed you on the campaigns we'll need. You've met our people. You understand that we're looking for a new, creative approach that will sell merchandise. We want to upgrade our image, get new outlets, dominate the market. We—to be frank—want miracles."

"I have a question," Murch said easily. "About fees. Would you people consider a one hundred per cent fee basis of payment to us rather than the usual fifteen per cent commission?"

A fleeting frown of annoyance crossed Mickels' face. "Why ... I ... we haven't thought much about that angle, Colton. We'd have to know more about it—give it some thought."

Pete glared a warning at Murch. "Virtually an academic question," he assured Mickels. "There's so much discussion about fee basis that we're sometimes curious to get reactions from—"

"It's more than that," Murch interrupted, smiling. "There's considerable thought that the fee basis creates a much better client-agency relationship. We're definitely interested in the idea."

"Now, Murch!" Pete protested. "Can't we work out some details about it so that Walt can have a better idea what we're talking about?"

"That's right," Mickels said. "It's pretty new. Why don't you include it in the material you give us about yourself? A point for discussion." He appeared to be uncertain about his stand.

"All right," Murch conceded. He glanced at Bill Rhodes and Mike McPherson. "Any special questions?" he asked them.

Bill said to Mickels: "I take it you'd like us to dream up some themes for the campaigns you briefed us on?"

"Right," Mickels said, obviously glad to drop the fee-basis discussion. "Something fresh—give us something that really *sings!*"

"We'll come up with some fresh copy slants," Bill assured him.

Mickels nodded emphatically. "I'm certain you will. And, incidentally, I hope you use your attractive little copywriter on this!"

"Linda Smith? You know her?"

"Met her at a cocktail party recently," Mickels said. "One of the magazine reps threw it. Waste of time if it weren't for your Linda. Damned attractive gal. Not married, is she?"

"No," Bill said quietly. "She's rather new in the business."

"Well, I hope you'll let her work on this," Mickels said. He looked at Mike McPherson. "Any questions, Mike?"

"Will it be all right if I check back with your designers and ask a few questions? So I can get the true feel of your creations?"

Mickels frowned again. "That poses a small problem. I appreciate your desire to get information and stuff with which to work, but I hate to infringe on our designers' time—" He shrugged apologetically. "You know how they are—temperamental. Perhaps we'd better have one person at your agency clear all this with me and I'll make arrangements for contacts. Sort of set up—well, let's call it a temporary account executive while you get your presentation ready."

"That makes sense," McPherson agreed.

"Okay," said Mickels, his decision made. "Pete. I suggest we have Pete act in that capacity. You clear with him and he can clear with me." He glanced at Murch and Bill. "Satisfactory?"

Pete made a protesting gesture, but without vigor. "Maybe Murch would like to—"

"No," Murch said. "That'll be fine."

"Pete and I are old friends," Mickels said. "It'll probably be easier working that way for the time being."

Murch grinned and stood up. "Speaking of work—I have to get back to the shop. Coming, Pete, or do you want to stay and chat with Walt?"

"It's almost lunchtime," Pete said. "Why don't we all go downtown and—"

"I'm sorry," Mickels said. "I've appointments right after one. If I go down, I'll be late. Why don't you people be my guests out here?"

"I'll take a rain check," Murch said. He looked at Bill and Mike. They nodded.

"Then how about you, Pete?" Mickels insisted.

"I'll take you up on that," Pete said. "We haven't had a chance to catch up on old times for a hell of a spell." He glanced at Murch. "Okay?"

"Certainly," Murch said and held out a hand to Mickels. "Thanks for your help, Walt."

"That's my job," Mickels said. He sat down at the table again and Pete took the chair across from him. The other three left the cafeteria.

"I *wondered* why Pete insisted upon bringing his car when we could all have come in yours," Bill said. "Now I know. Smart man."

Too damned smart, Murch thought, but he didn't say anything. He simply exchanged another glance with Bill. They both were thinking the same thing. Ahead of them Mike McPherson was striding briskly, head up, already mentally creating layouts.

Back at the agency Murch went directly to his office. He wanted to think through the things that were happening in the shop.

Before he could get settled at his desk the door opened and Bill Rhodes looked at him inquiringly. Murch waved him in and the thin, sandy-haired copy chief closed the door and took the client's chair beside Murch's desk.

"What's the pitch?" Bill asked.

"Which pitch?"

"Rhymes, yet! You know what I mean. Or shall we play a game of truth? The truth being that I'm on your side, Murch. Do I smell ambition on Pete?"

"I think you do," Murch said. "But remember—he owns part of the agency."

"You mean it's none of my business?"

"No. You work here. Everything that happens here is some of your business."

"You're an unusual employer, Murch," Bill said. "I guess that's why I stay around."

"How was the vacation trip?"

"I went, I saw and I came home."

"Kate?"

"I forget you know my past. I saw her."

"And?"

"Madison Avenue in skirts. She's made it big, Murch. But you know that. You read *Advertising Age*, too."

Murch nodded thoughtfully. He suspected that Bill still loved his ex-wife. Men and women. Husbands and wives. What about husbands and mistresses? And he thought instantly of Lorrie. He forced his mind into other channels. Bill was watching him with a curious smile, almost as if he had guessed Murch's short excursion into contemplation.

Murch said, "What do you think of the presentation idea?"

"Mike's so high on Cloud Nine, and Pete is so busy impressing the prospective client, that I only got a shirttail image of the idea. I gather we're going to put on nothing short of a spectacular. That it?"

Murch grinned. "In a manner of speaking."

"And Mike does some fancy art work for backgrounds—stage settings, so to speak? Probably incorporating some of the stuff we saw today?"

Again Murch nodded.

"And I write it?"

"You write it," Murch agreed.

"Who plays it?"

"Not Mike. He gets carried away. Pete can get too enthusiastic and sometimes he gets corny. We'll have to get someone solid to pitch for us, and each of us chime in on cue with our part in the agency. But we use a strong character to carry the full pitch."

"A sort of master of ceremonies."

"Right."

"Won't they wonder why we go outside for someone to pitch? Why we don't pitch our own bill of goods?"

"Nice questions," Murch said. "But I think we get around them by pointing out that we're an agency that's not afraid to hire good talent to supplement our regulars for special occasions. They'll understand that. They go outside to high-price free lancers for some of their styling."

"You're probably right. By the way, we're really working to impress Sam Gortzein, aren't we?"

"I think we are," Murch said, nodding thoughtfully. "But we'll have to please Mickels, too. If we angled the account over his head, and he had to work with us later, he could murder us. I've seen that happen."

"Anyhow, it looks as if Pete's taking care of Mickels," Bill said pointedly.

"Looks that way."

The tired-looking copy chief thoughtfully lit a cigarette. "Level with me, Murch. Do we need the LeLane's account as much as I think?"

Murch was not surprised that Bill knew the truth.

"As much as you think," he said.

"Douglas Lumber is not too solid," Bill said flatly. "You know that."

Murch shrugged. "Nothing definite. They may sell out. Just hints. Meanwhile, let's concentrate on LeLane's."

"Do we play along with Pete and Mike?"

"Yes. We've nothing to lose, Bill. I haven't a better idea. Have you? If you do, tell me now. I'm not buying because I like it particularly—it's because I think it's the best idea we have right now."

"It's a good idea," Bill said. "I'll do my best. We'd better think about talent. We'll need a man who is strong—who can get their attention and hold it."

"What's that old sales rule of yours, Bill?"

Bill grinned. "A-I-D-A. Attention—get their attention ... Interest—arouse their interest. Desire—build their desire for the product. Action—off to the store to buy!"

"Well, we need a guy named Aida—and that's a gal's name."

"But a man's job, in this case."

"Okay. One other thing—see if you can work your gal Friday into this. Obviously Linda has some talent and Mickels likes her. Don't get me wrong—we're only interested in selling her *talent*."

"Mickels is a wolf," Bill said. "And I get what you mean. We might prostitute the talent, but not the girl."

"Check."

They smiled at one another, almost thoughtfully, and Bill stood up to leave.

"Now you know where I stand, Murch," he said.

"I always knew," said Murch.

Bill returned to his small private office. Adjoining it, with a door between, was the even smaller office—hardly more than a cubbyhole—that was occupied by his single copywriter, Linda.

As he crossed to his desk he heard her typing busily. He sat down, and after a few moments the typing in the next office stopped. There was a short pause, as if she was reading the copy in her machine, and then the ratchet-whirr of the paper being pulled from the machine and the noise of her chair being pushed back from her desk.

He heard her come to the open doorway and he looked up. She wore a short, tight skirt and a sweater that looked expensive. She smiled, and he realized how pretty she was, enjoying again the crisp blueness of her eyes and the naturally blond hair. She filled out the sweater youthfully and excitingly, and the skirt could never do anything but compliment the trimness of her figure.

"Come in," he said.

She sat on one corner of his cluttered desk and looked down at him. He tried to keep his eyes away from the pleasant female line of her hip and thigh so close to him.

"Well?" she asked, her voice tense with hidden excitement. "Do you think there's a chance?"

"Could be," he said.

"Can I help with the presentation, Bill?" she asked eagerly.

"Murch wants you to help. As a matter of fact, the LeLane's people suggested it, too. They've noticed you. That's a nice compliment, gal."

She grinned and shook her head. "Depends," she said. "I met Walt Mickels at one of those rep parties. There's a glint in his eye, if you know what I mean. So I understand that. But have they noticed any of my fashion copy?" She blushed suddenly. "I mean—that must have sounded awful! Why should they notice any of my copy for The Smart Shop? Those little retail ads! I just mean that there's more than one way in which a girl can be interesting and—" She stopped speaking when she saw the amusement in Bill's eyes and joined his small laugh. "I'd better shut up," she said.

"We're having a meeting in the morning. We'll get into the presentation then. If you've anything hanging fire, you'd better clean up as much as you can this afternoon. It's going to be a busy shop for a while."

"It's exciting!"

"It's one hell of a big headache," Bill told her. "But I guess it's exciting, too. Maybe that's why we stay in the lousy business."

"Don't call it lousy, Bill! I don't want to be disillusioned. Not by *you*."

"I detect a small compliment somewhere in that, but I'll ignore it. Seriously, Linda, it's a good business."

"I love it!"

"You're developing into a good copywriter," he told her seriously.

"I hope so, Bill. I want to be good at it."

"Fine. I've built up your ego—so scram back into your cave. I have to make like a creative genius!"

She laughed and went back toward her office. She hesitated in the doorway.

"Bill?" she asked. "Did Murch really ask for me to work on the presentation?"

He looked up and for a second was almost startled by the intent expression on her face.

"Yes," he said. "Definitely. Before I got a chance."

Her face lit up in a warm smile. "Oh—I'm glad," she said, going into her office and closing the door after her.

Bill stared at the door thoughtfully. *I wonder if that kid has a yen for Murch?* he asked himself. *That look on her face—*

In her small office Linda sat at her typewriter and flipped a sheet of paper beneath the roller, but she didn't type. Instead, she gazed at the white paper, thinking about Murch Colton.

Sometimes she had to remind herself that Murch and Bill probably were about the same age, yet in her mental evaluations of the two men, she always seemed to think of Bill as being definitely middle-aged, worn and tired—the "old pro" who was more of a father image to her than anything else. He taught her how to write copy. He taught her how to sell through words and space and time. He guided her through the intricacies of learning the agency business and advertising. From him she acquired her job skills, her philosophy of copywriting, and her understanding of agency functions.

Murch was something else. He was not middle-aged in her mental image. He was "mature" rather than "older." He was exciting. He was symbolic of the vast world of *advertising.*

Even more than that, she admitted to herself honestly. *He does something to me. As a* man. *He excites* me. *He has power and drive and he knows—whatever it is that makes men different, it's the something that you realize the* different *ones* know. *He would* know *how to love a woman. He would* know *how to handle a situation.*

All her comparatively short life, Linda Smith consistently had made a game of evaluating people, and usually in terms of what they could do for her.

Just recently turned 23, Linda had come from a southern Oregon town where her father had a small business. She was the third in a family of five children. In school she had consistently made the honor roles scholastically because this was part of her early conceived plan. In her freshman year she had become associated with the high-school newspaper and she had found her talents almost at once. She could write. Her English teacher and other students assured her of that.

She followed the impetus of the high-school conditioning to take journalism at one of the smaller West Coast colleges. There she had learned much from an obliging professor and from a few older students who had worked on newspapers during summer months. The world of advertising came to her attention. The "good" money for writers—if they weren't tops in fiction, nonfiction, theater, television or the movies—was in advertising. She learned, too, that many free-lance writers earned the more substantial share of their income in copywriting jobs.

Her appraisal convinced her that she preferred to turn her journalistic skills—such as they were—toward advertising. She had sought a job and found it. Now she was learning and she had plans for the future. She had no doubt that she would accomplish all she wanted. She always had.

She had decided to become class president in her high school junior year. She had managed it. She had decided to go with the football captain in her senior year. She had managed it. She had also managed to take the lead in the school operetta that year.

In college she had carefully and relentlessly planned her activities. She again had managed a class presidency, other honors, and she had kept her dating schedule busier than most girls. She had decided early in life that she would keep a "good" reputation, a "fresh and innocent" appearance, but she would also learn *all* that she could about "life" as *soon* as she could.

She had yielded her virginity to the football captain. At college she had entered into a brief affair with a young, unmarried instructor who consequently worried about having "seduced" her on a winter night when she had managed to slip into his secluded apartment. Actually she had gone with the intention of being seduced. She had to *know*—always, *to know*. Neither set of sexual experiences had enthralled her, but she felt that they prepared her. She was knowledgeable.

She lived alone in a small apartment at the foot of the heights where apartments, built into old family mansions, could occasionally be found. These apartments were "good addresses" and close to the center of town. This saved bus fare, and she couldn't afford a car. She bought her clothes carefully, watching the sales.

She saved regularly because she knew that sooner or later she would need a sizable amount of money in order to make a change. She dated casually, sometimes for company and simply because it often meant dinner along with companionship. Most of the men she dated were from the "trade." She drank with them, discreetly. She went to the usual parties advertising people attended; to the symphony, ballet, foreign films, and to night clubs with dates.

Once in a great while she was tempted to sleep with one or the other of the pleasant, sparkling, sophisticated young advertising men she met. She had managed to resist the urge, however. Somehow she had a vague feeling that such things became known, one way or the other, in this fast-paced, literate group. If she was going to venture into sexual areas again, she must do it carefully and with a purpose.

Now, sitting at her typewriter and staring at the blank sheet of paper, she thought of these things and suddenly she knew she would go to bed with Murch Colton if he asked her. In fact, she wanted to go to bed with him—for many reasons.

The thought gave her a disturbing, alien warmness and she felt an awakening of her body that she seldom experienced or encouraged. For a moment she shut her eyes and thought how it would be. She *knew*. She knew exactly how it would start, but there was always the exciting question of how it would continue and where it would end.

She opened her eyes and lit a cigarette. She had to write five TV spots. She had to get her thoughts away from Murch and the possibilities and where that might lead.

After a few moments she began to type. Among other things, she also had learned discipline—especially when she was after something she wanted, and there were a great many things that Linda Smith wanted desperately.

CHAPTER FOUR

HELEN VAUGHAN, the competent thirtyish secretary who supervised the major secretarial and general detail in the agency, gave instructions to the girl at the small switchboard that all principals would be in the conference room this morning. With her usual competence she would take urgent calls during the two-hour "creative session" Murch had called.

In the conference room Murch was talking to the assembled staff. He sat at one end of the table. Bill and Linda occupied one side. Mike McPherson and Lorrie sat at the opposite side. Pete Lanham was at the other end.

The table was littered with sketches, sheets of suggested copy, ash trays, coffee cups. The air was heavy with cigarette smoke, and windows had been opened from the top. The men had discarded jackets and ties. The two women wore cool summer clothing.

"Let's sort this out," said Murch. He looked around at the others. They nodded. "I'd like to revert straight back to Bill's old A-I-D-A formula. Attention, interest, desire, and action. We can apply it to this presentation."

Pete lit another cigarette. "I was about to suggest that."

Murch smiled slightly. "Okay. The beginning. How do we get their attention?" He glanced at Bill who immediately took over the theme.

Bill said, "Murch can open with introductions and then launch the pitch. Or we can do a gimmick thing—which I don't favor. We need to show a *solid* image as well as a *fresh* one. Murch is the president of the agency. He can start the ball rolling."

Mike McPherson cleared his throat and said, "Pete should open things. He knows Mickels so well—he could ease into the whole thing and then introduce Murch as the president, then the rest of us, and finally our outside talent—and the show is on the road."

A brief silence followed his suggestion. From opposite ends of the table Murch and Pete smiled at one another inscrutably.

"What do you think, Pete?" Murch asked.

Pete Lanham shrugged and frowned. "You're president."

Bill Rhodes quickly said, "That's right. Murch *is* the president—it's logical that he opens the session. Let's set it that way." He glanced at the others. Lorrie and Linda nodded. Mike looked annoyed.

Pete Lanham knocked ashes from his cigarette and said, "Okay. How do we catch their attention fast? How will you hook them?"

Bill said, "I understand that we present to Gortzein, Mickels, the sales, promotional and production department heads. Even some company directors. A fair-sized audience."

"Everybody but the relatives!" said Pete.

Murch said, "With a sizable audience you can create atmosphere, mood, excitement."

"So?" asked Lanham.

"So I open by thanking them for the opportunity to make a presentation. I say that it is important that they get an accurate and comprehensive image of us as an agency. Therefore, we have taken a leaf from techniques we've used for our clients—we are employing top, proved media to present our story. But also I impress upon them that *we* have written the copy, created the art, and conceived the sell. Then I introduce our outside talent and he goes into his pitch."

Murch stopped talking and waited for comments.

Pete put out a cigarette and lit another thoughtfully. "When do you introduce the staff?"

"After the pitch."

"Why not before?"

"They'll be more interested in meeting the staff if they like what they've seen. If we haven't been effective, we'll have missed anyhow, so it won't make any difference."

"Sounds a little theoretical," Pete said.

"No," Bill said. "It makes sense."

Pete shrugged. "Let's get on. Who introduces the act isn't very important anyhow. Mike and I have dreamed up some things. We'd like your reactions."

Bill said to Murch, "Mike has shown me some stuff for copy slants. I think we need to pull it together."

Murch suppressed a smile. Bill was giving him the ball whenever he could. Murch said, "Outside of routine qualifications—financial responsibility, size of staff, standing in the trade—we have two important things to punch. First, what we've done for others; our experience and past performance. Second, what we can do for LeLane's. Make sense?"

Almost grudgingly, Pete nodded. "That's the way Mike and I have been thinking."

Mike McPherson spoke, his voice eager: "And we can make a *dramatic* presentation of what we've done for others. I mean, we present cold, hard facts *dramatically*! And as for what we can do for *them*, we really go into outer space—"

"All flavored with hard sell," Pete hastily supplemented. "Mike has some ideas about their styling, fabrics, and doing some effective treatments."

"One point," interrupted Murch. "Let's not overlook the novelty of having this pitch made by some real masculine guy. It's new and different to have a hunk of male sex appeal pitching a women's line. We pick up the old theory that women dress for men—whether they do or not. It makes sense that a woman will listen to a male powerhouse admiring merchandise that *she* could wear. And certainly it will be a novelty for LeLane's to see their stuff pitched by a rugged he-man."

"We might suggest a complete campaign tied to such a guy," said Pete. "We could do worse."

"Could be," Murch said.

"Then we're all agreed that we go on my idea—and Mike's?" Pete asked.

"Yes," Murch said. "Bill, Linda—I want good copy. You two work with Mike and Lorrie. If you want to do a Broadway production to be effective, then do it. But no corn. No phony hoopla. I don't think Old Man Gortzein would buy it."

"Exactly," said Pete Lanham. "And about the qualifications, Murch—a bound booklet for them? Financial statement, credit— all that stuff?"

"You and I can work it up," said Pete.

Bill asked, "How about visuals: film, slides, flipboards?"

Mike said archly, "When I'm ready I'll discuss them with you. You can begin the copy part without visual essentials."

Bill gazed levelly at the artist. "All right, Mike. But remember that we must have something before we can tie it together."

Linda looked at Lorrie, and the older woman gave the young copy-writer a warm smile.

"It'll work out just fine," Lorrie. "Linda and I will handle the distaff angles."

"Wonderful!" said Murch, getting up to break the small tension. "Let's go." He looked at Pete and added, "Maybe you and I should get on the qualifications stuff."

The conference was ended earlier than Murch had antici-pated. Meanwhile the routine work of the agency must be con-tinued. As usual, a presentation was extra work that frequently called for late hours, wearied bodies, and frayed nerves.

Just before the two agency heads separated, Pete said, "Any ideas about talent for the pitch? The guy we'll use?"

"No," Murch said. The problem worried him. He didn't want to go to Holywood for talent. It would be expensive. Furthermore, selection of the right man was important. It would be too easy to miss with the wrong man.

As Murch anticipated, Pete had a suggestion: "I could make a fast trip to Hollywood. I've connections there."

"Let's wait until we get the the script firmed."

"We don't want to louse this one," Pete said testily.

"We won't," Murch said quietly. His eyes locked with Pete's.

"Okay. Only I know Mickels pretty well. He isn't easy to impress and we're pitching against big league stuff."

"We all know that," Murch said. He left the smaller man and returned to his own office where he thumbed through telephone notations Helen had placed on his desk. He stopped with one and dialed the Douglas Lumber number and hung up with relief a few moments later. The call had been unimportant, but he never knew when a call from the lumber company might prove other-wise. Idly he wondered if they would call him or write him if they sold out and terminated the account.

A soft tap on the door sounded. He called out an invita-tion to enter. Lorrie came in, closed the door, and leaned back against it.

"A good meeting," she said. "But there's friction between you and Pete, isn't there?"

"It shows?"

"Of course. But you were objective."

"Do you like the ideas?"

"It's a good pitch," she said. "Not as world-shaking as Mike thinks, but he has some good ideas."

"Is he giving you anything to do, Lorrie? I want you in this."

She nodded. "He wants me to work on stuff for suggested campaigns—the styling and fabrics bit: a gay, modern, go-every-where-in-LeLane's feeling; wind-in-the-hair for the casuals; Styled-for-the-setting in other things."

"You can do it," Murch said with authority.

"I hope so," Lorrie said. "Incidentally, does the agency make call reports?"

He nodded. "After every call upon a client. A memo copy goes to everyone concerned, reviewing what was said and decided during the call."

"Ones I used to see from other agencies sometimes said: 'If there are discrepancies or corrections, please notify us at once.' Or something like that."

Murch looked into her green-blue eyes and saw a sparkle in them, as if she was about to break into a smile.

She said, "May I have a call report on the other night?"

He got up from behind the desk and came around it to face her. He put one hand on the door beside her head and leaned his weight against the panel. He looked down into her face.

"Nothing has changed," he said softly. "Only intensified." He deliberately and carefully pressed his mouth to hers. Her lips were quiet and then slightly active for an instant. The couple drew back from the kiss, smiling.

"Thank you," Murch said.

"I'd better get back to work. I was just checking."

"Lorrie," he said softly. "We'd better—"

"Later," she interrupted. "Mike's waiting."

He opened the door and watched her walk down the hallway, again masculinely pleased by the feminine rise and fall of buttocks, the swing of hips and legs, and again suddenly wanting her with acute physical awareness.

He watched her go into Mike's office. Farther down the hallway Pete came out of an office with papers in his hand and headed toward Murch.

"Got time to check the financial statement now?" Pete said.

"Yes," Murch said, turning back into his office. He found a cleansing tissue and hastily wiped his lips.

At approximately the same time that the staff meeting was in session, Diana Colton awakened in her bed in the beach apartment. For a few moments she listened to the roar of the surf with eyes closed, body relaxed, luxuriating in a sense of well-being and deep, restful sleep that follows sexual satiation.

Rick Andes had left her bed in the early morning hours, and now she was alone in her nudity beneath the sheet and light blanket he had pulled over her. She stretched and realized that he had left evidences of his love-making. Her thigh muscles were sore. Her body felt used, but it was not an unpleasant feeling. The soreness and aches only recalled the essence of his masculinity and domination in his love-making.

"Mistress," she told herself. "Diana, mistress to Rick."

She faced her unfaithfulness to Murch, and was slightly shocked that she felt no guilt.

There's no love left for Murch, she thought *It's been over longer than I knew. Or maybe it just died. How do I know? Or should I? Men like Rick just happen to a woman.*

She got out of bed, smiling at her nightgown trailing over a chair, where he had thrown it the night before. It had been a useless gesture even to wear it, she thought. She got into a robe and put coffee on and then bathed.

Rick was going deep-sea fishing and wouldn't be back until night. She had the day to herself, and she decided to drive into Douglas City to shop. She felt a need for new beach clothes, now that Rick would be with her.

She quickly finished her breakfast, tidied the apartment, and was on the highway a little after ten. It was a beautiful day that promised to be hot. She drove without haste, thinking about Rick Andes and what he had brought to her.

Never before had she experienced the complete release he had brought her, nor the exciting sense of subjugation. Vividly she remembered the cupping strength of his hands beneath her, the relentless taking, and his obvious pleasure in fulfilling her needs before he found his own almost furious release.

Before she realized it, she was on the outskirts of the city. She drove through traffic and stopped at the house. Quickly she skimmed through accumulated mail and then went to the master bedroom and packed some lingerie—garments that Rick Andes might find exciting.

Momentarily she debated about letting Murch know she was in town, and decided she should. If she shopped downtown someone they knew might see her and mention it to him. She dialed the agency.

"Have lunch with me," he suggested.

"Will you be able to return to the beach, Murch?"

"I doubt it. We'll talk it over."

She arrived at the agency shortly before noon. She looked in to say hello to Mike and was surprised to find Lorrie at work.

"They've drafted me," Lorrie explained. "How's the beach?"

"Wonderful," Diana said. "I pity you slaves!"

"We envy you," Mike said. "With your tan you could model for outdoor casuals."

"No, thank you, Mike," she told him. "I'm not the long-legged, breezy, outdoor type. Use your wife. Lorrie, you're everything I used to wish I'd be when I was a growing girl."

Lorrie shook her head. "That trim, compact figure of yours is called the real package deal."

They were good, but not close friends. Lorrie held no envy for this wife of Murch Colton, and she didn't believe that Diana actually envied her. Nor did she believe that Diana Colton was very much in love with Murch Colton.

Murch had heard his wife's voice and came down the hallway. He asked the McPhersons to join them at luncheon. Mike shook his head "We've promised to go with Pete. He wants to talk ideas."

Murch and Diana lunched at a nearby restaurant. She asked about the presentation. She was intelligent and knowledgeable about the business.

"It sounds wonderful," she said. Thoughtfully she picked up a glass of water. "Who is going to be your outside talent?"

"That's the big problem. We need a man. Pete wants to do the Hollywood bit, but I don't think it's necessary."

Diana tried to keep excitement out of her voice, but the idea had come to her instantly, and she liked all the ramifications.

"Rick Andes," she said.

Murch put down his fork and stared at her.

"Why didn't *I* think of him!" he exclaimed. "Sure! Everything we need. Ex-pro football star, a terrific talent on television—at least, that's what I hear. You've watched him?"

"Terrific," she said, thinking that the description extended far beyond the television screen.

"He's still at the beach?"

"I think so. I've chatted with him a few times."

"Look—when you get back ask him to call me. Or sound him out."

"He's exactly right for this, Murch!"

"We could even build a campaign around him for some of the garments—let him pitch them. An ex profootballer pitching women's casuals! Copy: 'Girls—know what a guy like me likes to see on gals like you. The casual, sun-loving, fun-loving, fashioned-for-femmes clothes that only LeLane's creates for you women!' "

Diana smiled, thinking how quickly Rick Andes had removed her clothes. What does Rick Andes like on girls? Nothing! Absolutely nothing!

Oddly, she was shocked by her Rabelaisian thought and knew that she was on the verge of blushing. But there was a wild, delightful, outrageous loss of inhibitions when she made love with Rick, or even thought about it.

"I'll talk with him," she said.

"There's no use hoping I can get back to the beach," he told her. "But there's no reason why you shouldn't stay a while longer."

She thought quickly. From things Rick had said, she knew he had considerable more time for vacationing. She didn't want to return to the city while he was there. If he took the agency assignment he undoubtedly would commute the few times necessary for him to be on hand.

"Then I'll stay on a while longer," she said. "While you're busy with the presentation you won't be home much, anyhow."

"Fine," he agreed. "Stay as long as you like—and I'll plan not to return. Maybe later I can grab another week or two."

Murch returned to the agency and Diana shopped for a new bathing suit, wondering if a bikini would be too daring for the quiet resort town. She decided to buy it.

An hour later she was headed back toward the beach. She thought about Rick Andes and wondered if he would be back from fishing in time to have dinner with her at the apartment. They could have some drinks, and dinner, and afterwards a long ride if it was a nice night, or a walk on the beach, or they could just stay in the apartment and listen to the sound of the surf as they lay on her bed.

She stepped on the gas as she smiled a small and secret smile of anticipation.

CHAPTER FIVE

M URCH RETURNED to the agency and announced his decision to try for Rick Andes. Even Pete approved, although he obviously was disappointed to abandon a trip to Hollywood.

During the remainder of the afternoon, work was intensified upon the pitch, and the more routine duties of the agency seemed to acquire a diminishing importance.

Shortly after three o'clock Linda came into Bill's office, looking amused and a little excited

"I just had a phone call," she said. "Mr. Mickels."

Bill glanced up sharply. The advertising man from LeLane's was moving quickly.

"Personal, I take it?" he said.

"Oh, *quite!* Would I have a drink and dinner with him after work? And maybe a show? There's a new Italian picture playing at Cinema 35."

"You're going?"

"Would it hurt anything if I did, Bill?"

He frowned. "Your life is your own. You don't have to ask us for permission to date."

"You sound almost ominous."

"Should I make like an older man with the advice?"

"Yes."

"He has a reputation."

"Now he does interest me!" she announced. "Don't you think reputations add allure to men?"

He laughed. "So that dates me. But he has a yen for you, and I know it and Murch does and Pete."

"Did he say something?" she asked inquisitively.

"That he'd met you. Complimentary."

She smiled sweetly. "I think I'll go. I can take care of myself, Bill, so don't worry. Maybe I can do something for the agency."

"The less you mention the agency, the better," he cautioned. "Outside of the Pentagon nothing is more classified than what goes on in an agency. Of course, all media people—even suppliers and delivery boys—seem to know what's happening, but it's still classified. Never get caught talking about what your agency is doing."

"I'd never say anything," she protested, sounding hurt.

"I know you wouldn't," he assured her. "Only Mickels might try to question you. I just wanted to warn you."

"And that he's a wolf, and has a reputation?"

"In a manner of speaking," he said solemnly. "And if you go to Cinema 35 with him after being wined and dined, and the picture is sexy, the risk is on your own head."

"You sound almost serious!"

"I am. I like you."

"I'll not play Mata Hari, or whatever they called her. And I won't give my all for our dear agency. I just hope he takes me to a good place for dinner. I'm virtually broke until payday."

"Mercenary wench," Bill said sadly.

The girl returned to her office and Bill swiveled around in his chair to face his typewriter again. He studied the opening to the presentation that he had just written. It sounded good. Abruptly he realized that it would be helpful if he knew which agencies would compete against them. He picked up the telephone and asked for Murch. Murch was out for coffee. He asked for Pete.

"Pete," he said, "I'm working up the pitch. It would be helpful if I knew who we're competing against. Did Mickels tell you?"

"I got it out of him," Pete said. "We go against Strath, Bond and Rase, from here. The nationals are a little rougher. All New York. Bye and Connors, Rausmeyer Associates, and—oh, oh! something just occurred to me. There's a personal angle here, Bill."

"Personal angle?" Bill asked quietly.

"The other agency—and probably the toughest—is Crescent, West and Cameron—CWC. Isn't that—?" He left the sentence unfinished.

"Yes," Bill said. "That's where my ex-wife heads up TV and radio. I wonder why they're interested in a small fashion house?"

"Probably because it *is* a small fashion house," Pete said. "Small, but a hell of a good name—and it's no schlock house. Maybe CWC is spreading out. They haven't touched the garment business before, have they?"

"I don't think so," Bill said thoughtfully. He did not like Pete especially, but he acknowledged that the small man was shrewd. And whatever was the reason for the large agency's interest in LeLane's, the disturbing element was that CWC *was* interested and would be competition. The most disturbing thought for Bill, of course, was Kate Rhodes and what part she might have in the presentation—if any.

His thoughts had brought on a short silence and Pete spoke almost sharply. "Any ideas about them?" he asked.

"Nothing world-shaking," Bill said.

"Did you see your ex-wife in New York?"

"Yes."

"What did you talk about? Did she mention pitching this account?"

It's none of your damned business what we talked about! Bill thought. Aloud he said, "We didn't discuss business."

"Well ... it was an idea," Pete said. "It'd be helpful if we knew what angle they'll take. Maybe she'll be out and you can snoop around a little."

"I doubt if she'll be here," Bill said shortly. "She wouldn't talk if she did come. And I wouldn't ask. We're still figuratively at swords' points. Besides, I don't think we need to do any spying. I don't have a trench coat for playing that bit."

"Christ! You do *anything* in this business, Bill! I want to know everything our competitors plan."

"Let it lay," Bill said easily. He didn't want an argument about business ethics. "We can pretty well figure them out. Our local competition will be staid, as usual. Bye and Connors will be conservative, talk big-magazine space. Rausmeyer Associates will try cuteness—the eye-patch angles. CWC can throw anything—balanced media selection and schedules, good campaign ideas. And they'll point up their vast experience in the women's market—all that soap and food experience they've had."

Pete grunted. "Okay," he said. "We'll talk more about it later." He hung up.

Bill slowly put down his telephone and thought about the information he had received from Pete Lanham. The news that CWC was competing bothered him. It was a powerful, alert agency that billed in millions. They would spend money to get the LeLane's account, and they had top talent and research facilities.

After lunch, Murch had tried to concentrate on work, but by three o'clock he began to feel the first twinges of a headache creeping from the back of his neck to behind his eyes. This was a tension headache and he was wise enough to recognize it. He left the office and got his car from the parking lot.

He drove across town to the Douglas Lumber offices, but the advertising manager was out. He made a few routine calls on other accounts. He had no business of importance to transact at any place, but the calls served to keep him busy. In the back of his mind he wrestled with the problem of the presentation, and the problems of the agency.

It was close to five o'clock when he made his last call. He spotted a telephone booth and stopped to call the agency. There had been no urgent calls for him. Upon an impulse he asked to speak with Mike McPherson.

The art director answered the call. He sounded annoyed with the interruption.

Murch said, "Mike, I thought you and Lorrie might eat downtown with me tonight. Diana went back to the beach. You could fill me in on what you've done on the pitch."

"Not tonight, Murch," McPherson said. "I have a committee meeting. Art Museum Association. It's a dinner thing."

"Then how about Lorrie? I hate to eat alone."

"She'd probably like that. I'll let you ask her."

Lorrie's voice came over the wire. "Mike says you'll buy my dinner!"

Murch said, "Hotel cuisine or a hamburger joint?"

"H-m-m. The hamburger—if it's at the drive-in on Sky Road. I love theirs."

"Be in front of the building in ten minutes."

"I'll be there."

He was suddenly glad he had made the date. He hadn't expected to see Lorrie alone, and actually had intended to question Mike about the pitch. Now he would have Lorrie to himself, and she would know as much about what Mike was doing as Mike, himself, would know.

She was waiting for him, looking tall, slim and smart. The late afternoon sun brought glints to her hair, and the gray streak looked alluring. She smiled as she got into the car.

"It's hot!" she said.

"It'll be better up on the Sky Road," he said. "Rough day?"

"No. A fun day. The pitch is beginning to make sense."

"Tell me."

Briefly she reviewed the day's accomplishments. Murch nodded occasionally. The pitch was shaping up.

"I didn't get a chance to ask you," he said. "What do you think of Rick Andes as our pitchman?"

"Marvelous! I've watched his show. He has something. He projects."

"I hope we can get him."

"When will you know?"

"Diana will see him this evening, probably. I'll call her after we eat."

He picked his way swiftly through the after-work traffic to Sky Road and began to climb behind the city, through shaded canyons formed by towering fir trees.

At the top of the grade the highway leveled out and wound along the mountain ridge. The countryside was spread below them. When they turned into the drive-in, they decided against eating in the car and got out and went to a table on a sprawling patio.

They ordered hamburgers and ate with pleasure. The food was exceptionally good. The coffee was fresh and rich in flavor. The smell of the forest was about them, and the heat of a hot summer day still lingered in brassy emphasis.

He looked across the table at her, seeing the green-blue eyes and the beat of a pulse in her throat. She was an exciting woman, he thought. Exciting and desirable.

"Can we talk about us?" he suddenly asked.

"Is there any need?"

"You don't think so?"

She shook her head. "We don't have to say it. When two persons know, they don't have to talk about it."

"I'm just beginning to know you," he said thoughtfully. "I've never known another woman like you."

"I don't believe you've known many other women."

"That's a word worth thinking about," he smiled. "To *know* a woman—to *know* a man. There was the old Biblical meaning. To know a woman was to make love to her. It's not a bad use of the word. How else to better know a woman—or a man?"

"In many other ways, Murch. But I understand what you mean. Are we going to make Kinsey-report talk now?"

He laughed. "I want to know you," he said.

She nodded. "Someday you will." She looked at him silently and her smile returned. "I shan't be brazen," she finally said. "But I shall be honest."

"I want us both to be honest."

"I have to look after Mike a little. I mean … there's almost a matronly responsibility, and it doesn't especially become me. Only I can't help having it."

"He doesn't make you a good husband or—" Murch hesitated. He had almost said "lover."

"No, Murch. He doesn't fulfill. I am never replete. Is that what you mean?"

He nodded.

"For some women it wouldn't make much difference," she said. "For me it does, and I can't help it. We can have trouble controlling our bodies and emotions and needs. To me, *sublimation* is a very vague word. *Frustration* is a very poignant word. Murch, I'm a woman—a very warm and mature woman. I need, and want, and sometimes I crave. It's not something I can turn off or on like an electric light. It glows steadily and deeply within me and sometimes it flames and soars and even rages. I shouldn't tell you this."

"You *should* tell me. I understand it."

She laughed softly and shook her head. "Not all, Murch. Some of this is beyond a man's understanding: the matronly concern I have for Mike, or how deep the glow can be, or how high the flame. It's so simple for a man. Some of it. Love-making, for instance. It can come to such a logical completion for him because it's ... it's *mechanical.* For a woman it's more than that. We can't always be certain. And, of course, there are men who aren't as capable as they might be."

She shuddered. "Let's not talk about it, Murch. Sometimes it seems almost unclean. I feel dirty. I hate what I think." Her eyes seemed to go beyond him into deep introspection. "Sometimes I admit to myself that I am married to a homosexual, who only occasionally can function as a heterosexual, and then inadequately. This is a terrible thing to tell you, Murch. I shouldn't. But I think you want to talk about us. Maybe it's better if we do. And you?"

"I don't know," he said slowly. "Diana ... ? I don't know if there ever was anything really there. The values we have today are never the ones we had five, ten, fifteen years ago. And if you don't keep pace together, there isn't much left after a while. There isn't for Diana and me."

"We're being very honest, aren't we?" she said.

"Yes. Lorrie ... when will I *truly* know you?"

"Not yet. I have to get used to the idea. I've realized for a long time that it was likely to happen for us, but now that we're talking about it, I have to get used to the idea. Make sense?"

"Not particularly, but I don't mind. Will you come down to my house while I phone Diana to find out about Andes?"

She shook her head. "No. You're really asking me if I'll go home with you to bed. Let's not clutter things unnecessarily. We can wait a while longer."

"All right. I'll take you home. But now—before we leave this table—listen to me once more. I want you ... you're beautiful, exciting, and a woman. A beautiful woman. I love you." He looked into her eyes and they both smiled and nodded a little as if they had agreed upon a pact.

He drove her home and said good night at the curb. For a moment their hands touched and then she turned and hurried toward her door.

He went home, opened the doors and windows to let a whisper of an evening breeze stir through the house, and in the den he put in a call for Diana. She answered at the beach apartment.

"Murch?" she asked. "I hoped it would be you. I just had dinner with Rick and gave him your message. We came here and we've been trying to get you. Shall I put him on?"

"You sound triumphant!"

She laughed softly. "Here's Rick."

The man's voice was crisp and rich. "Hi, Murch. I think your gal made a sale."

"Wonderful! I don't know what your fee is, but if it's reasonable, we have a deal."

"How much time is involved?"

Briefly Murch outlined the idea and the part that Andes would play.

"It'll take some rehearsal time," Murch concluded. "And, of course, the presentation itself. How much?"

Andes named a fee. Murch thought it was a trifle high, but he accepted promptly. The presentation deserved some expense.

"When do we start?" Andes asked.

"Day after tomorrow? Afternoon? We could at least get cleared away."

"Fine. I'll be there."

After he had hung up, Murch dialed Bill Rhodes. Bill answered at once and received Murch's news with enthusiasm.

Murch asked, "Will we have enough to start him after tomorrow?"

"We should have." Bill gave him a quick rundown on his day's accomplishemnts, as well as the news about Mickel's approach to Linda.

"I hope she doesn't get into something there," Murch said. "You know Mickels."

"I warned her and she says she can handle him."

"Hope so. Incidentally, did Pete tell you about CWC?"

"Yes. I don't think they'll send Kate out, but she might guess how I'd work up a pitch for you. That worries me a little."

"Forget it. Get a good sleep."

He had barely put down the telephone when Lorrie called. "I couldn't wait," she said. "Did you get Diana?"

"It's all set. Andes is buying."

"I'm so glad!"

"So am I. And thanks again for having dinner with me."

"I talk too much."

"We'll see," he said softly. "Soon … I hope."

At a little after midnight Linda Smith put down her drink as the last strains of a record sounded on the hi-fi speakers in Walter Mickels' apartment. For the first time she wished she had not accepted his invitation for a drink at his place after the show. He was beside her on a low, sprawling divan and the movie at

Cinema 35 *had* been sexy and it—or something—had given Walt Mickels some ideas.

She had let him kiss her casually. Now she quickly and firmly removed a hand that had crept to her breast. She leaned forward and put her drink on a coffee table.

"I'd better be going," she said. "It's been a nice evening, Walt."

He didn't attempt to replace the errant hand, and he smiled slightly. He acted as if he knew all the lines of this play and was content to let the action unfold according to the script; possibly if not tonight, some other night. Only a man should always start by trying.

"We're adults," he said simply.

"Of course. That's why it's time for me to go. We don't want to get involved."

"Why not?" he challenged, returning her smile.

"Lots of reasons, Walt—the agency, Murch Colton …"

"Murch?" His eyebrows went up.

"Don't be silly, Walt. Not *that.*"

"It has to be *someone,*" he teased. "You're much too lovely and desirable for there not to be *someone.*"

"I'm glad you didn't say 'available.' It would have ended a beautiful friendship."

"Don't be touchy, Linda. Not with me. I'm what I am, and you've probably been warned. But you needn't worry. Only I always hate to see two intelligent, modern, and understanding persons pass up a golden opportunity."

"Now you are pressing!" She laughed and got up. He stood and suddenly took her in his arms and kissed her. For a few seconds she relaxed and returned his kiss, and then spun neatly away from him. It was an evasive maneuver that she had learned long ago.

"All right," he said, accepting defeat. "Home you go."

She felt relief. She had not been certain that he could be so conveniently handled. As they went down in the automatic elevator, he said, "Are you going to work on the presentation?"

She nodded. Contrary to Bill's expectations, this was the first mention Mickels had made of the agency.

"Good," he said. "We can talk about it next time. Maybe I can help you a little. After all, I *do* know what we like!"

This, she realized, was a more direct approach than it might seem. It was in the tone of his voice; subtly there, not wholly definitive. *But,* she thought, *if he's foolish enough to let me know what they like and I can use the tip in the pitch, doesn't that help the agency? Isn't this part of the business?*

"I always like to learn," she said gaily.

"Good. I'm a fair teacher."

The elevator stopped and they went out to his small foreign sports car. He drove her straight home and said good night without attempting to kiss her again, but there was a small, mocking look in his eyes.

She thanked him and heard his sports car whirr away from the curb in a typical ascension of gears. She went into her own small apartment and got ready for bed, thinking about the evening.

In bed with the lights out, she remembered the love scenes from the Italian movie, the feel of his lips on her mouth, and the touch of his hand on her breast.

As he had said, it had been an opportunity. But not with him. She thought of the men she had known and finally she thought of Murch. It could have been with him. She shut her eyes tightly and let her imagination carry her off into the fantasies of what might have happened if the man had been Murch.

Her hands moved and she breathed more quickly and finally she gasped softly. Then in an impatient flounce of displeasure with herself she turned on one side and very quickly she was asleep.

CHAPTER SIX

M URCH PUT HIS CAR in the parking lot and walked toward the agency. Even at eight in the morning it was hot, and the weatherman predicted a temperature above a hundred. The cool shower he had taken after arising was wearing off and he was beginning to feel the heat and the residual weariness of a restless night.

This was the day that Rick Andes would be in town. The preceding day had been almost frantic with activity as the agency had tried to firm up the presentation, and this morning Bill Rhodes was already at work, his typewriter clattering loudly. Murch stopped at the copy chief's office.

"How late did you work last night, Bill?" he demanded.

"I left a half-hour after you did. Then I couldn't sleep. I'm rewriting some of it."

"I know," Murch said wearily. "I did my own tossing and turning. I still don't know if we shouldn't build up our financial background."

"The main thing is whether or not we *look* all right financially. Frankly, I don't know."

"We're all right—as of now," Murch said.

"If we lose Douglas Lumber?"

"Then the picture isn't so good."

"The weakness of small agencies." Bill smiled ruefully.

Murch nodded. "It's a merry-go-round. You build a small agency on one or two big accounts that crack the nut for you.

Then you try to pick up more. You get more and then expenses go up, so you pressure to bring in even more business, and the whole damned thing starts all over again. Only sooner or later you lose one of your big accounts. Then if you don't have enough spread in other accounts to absorb the loss, you're in trouble."

"You need to be diversified," Bill said.

"That's difficult in a smaller community. Not enough big accounts. You start to pick up retail accounts and they really kill you! For instance, the main reason for Linda is The Smart Shop retail account, and the other small ones she works on. It's a salary we pay to service them. I'm not sure we make any money on them, if we count service time, production, Linda's, yours—hell, it's a rat race!"

"Linda's doing pretty well on other stuff," Bill said. "She's contributed a lot to the pitch. Has a real flair for fashion copy."

"You've a pretty good touch yourself," Murch told him.

Bill shook his head. "Just the old pro showing. But that doesn't make me a good women's fashion writer. I've a theory about that. I think the best women fashion writers are women— or pansies, latent or active. That let's me out on all counts. But that Linda gal—she's got the makings of a topflight fashion writer."

"That's an asset," Murch said. "We'll use as much of her stuff as you think is good, and play her up. Incidentally, how about that date she had with Mickels? Any repercussions?"

Bill shook his head. "Evidently he didn't make the big pass. She said she had a nice—and, she assured me—*innocent* time. He wasn't even too inquisitive about the agency."

"I still hope she wears her chastity belt when she's with him," Murch said. "He's a louse."

"I agree. Meanwhile, how about this afternoon? Are we going to do a first run-through on the pitch?"

"Do we have enough? Rick Andes is coming in. That helped keep me awake. I'm not sure if we're ready for him."

"By ten o'clock I'll have enough to start with. Mike has some roughs on the art stuff he wants to use. Lorrie has some really sweet stuff on campaign ideas. I mean, that girl has it.'

Instinctively Murch felt a touch of pride in Bill's sincere praise of Lorrie. "She's good," he agreed. "Bring in the copy when you have it. I wonder if Pete had the financial statement typed."

"I think so. He's been pinch-hitting in production. Christ! No one even seems to think about Harold! Do you know how he is?"

Murch nodded again. It was true. In the excitement of getting the presentation readied everyone seemed to have forgotten that the third principal of the firm, Harold Simpson, was in the hospital.

"I saw him yesterday," Murch said. "He's holding his own, but he won't be back soon. Maybe I ought to look for another production man to fill in.'

"Pete does fairly well, with Helen's help," Bill said. "Not too much going through now, anyhow."

Murch went on to his office. The air conditioning had made it too cool. He decided to open a window and let a little warm air in. When he turned, Lorrie was in his office.

"Hi," she said cheerfully. "Hot day!"

She wore a thin blouse and a linen skirt. She looked fresh and cool and very lovely, he thought.

"You're early," he commented. "Is Mike here, too?"

"He went out to LeLane's to get some garments and material swatches for one of his campaign ideas."

Murch walked to where she stood by the doorway. From down the hallway came the furious clatter of Bill's typewriter. No one else seemed to be in the office. Murch closed the door, pulled her into his arms ad kissed her hard and long, letting his hands feel the firm lines of her back. She returned the kiss without stint, and they were a little breathless when they stood apart.

"We shouldn't let that happen here," she said. "It's dangerous."

"I couldn't help it," he said.

"Rick Andes coming in today?" she asked, inspecting her lips in a handbag mirror. She carefully applied lipstick and handed him a piece of tissue. "There's some on your mouth," she told him.

"Rick will be in this afternoon," he said. "We'll have a walk-through. Tell Mike when he comes in."

"He won't miss it," she said. "He's excited about Andes being on the job. He admires him tremendously."

Something in her voice caught his attention. He looked at her closely, and she returned his gaze with complete candor.

"It could happen," she said. "He becomes terrifically attracted to some men—some types."

"I hardly think Rick Andes plays in that league."

"Of course not. But Mike ... well, I shouldn't talk about it."

"Why not? Aren't things pretty well settled between us? About Mike—you mean a latent thing?"

"Latent—sublimated—whatever you want to call it. I know it and he knows that I know it. Only knowing it doesn't make it any easier. And I see the expression on his face when he talks about Rick Andes."

"Let's not cross bridges."

"No. Only I have a feeling—I don't know, Murch, sometimes I'm frightened.'

"Don't be."

They heard Bill speak to someone and Helen Vaughan's voice sang out a "Good morning." The staff was arriving for work. Lorrie shrugged a little helplessly and smiled at him.

"We can talk later," she said. She left the office and he heard her greet Helen and one of the stenographers. He heard Linda's voice and then Pete Lanham's.

He went out and motioned to Pete. The short, bristling man came rapidly down the hallway, wearing his usual professional smile, and followed Murch into the office, closing the door after him. "Something special, Murch?" he asked.

Murch nodded and lit a cigarette. It tasted brassy. He was smoking too much, drinking too much coffee, driving too hard. He felt tired and sour.

"First," said Murch, "is Harold. We'd better realize it may be a few days longer before he can take a hand."

"I know," Pete said.

"Do you need any help handling production?"

"No, I can use Helen and there isn't too much going through."

Murch said briefly, "I just want to make certain. We can get someone in, if that's necessary.'

"I think not yet."

"Now, the second point. Mike is out at LeLane's getting garments and swatches. Is he clearing through you? As I recall, we made that arrangement with them. They were a little reluctant to have us bother their people. We've got to be careful."

"He cleared with me. I'm on top of it." The small man pushed his glasses more firmly against the bridge of his nose, a habit he had when he was annoyed. When pressed to outright anger, he usually removed the glasses.

"As long as he cleared," Murch said quietly. The curtain of invisible antagonism was between them again. He smashed his cigarette out in an impatient gesture.

"And point number three?" Pete asked curtly, pressing his glasses again with a forefinger.

"Last night I took home your draft of the booklet covering our financial condition and the other guff. It's a good job, Pete."

Lanham pressed the glasses again. "Okay," he said. "It's a good job, *but*—and what's the 'but' that's bothering you?"

"I didn't see any mention of a service fee instead of the usual commission deal. Why isn't it there, Pete?"

"Because I think it's a lot of crap," Pete Lanham retorted in a grating, vulgar voice. Now he took off his glasses and glared at Murch with angry eyes that looked strangely naked and childish without the big black rims. "So shall we make an issue of it, Murch?"

"Why not? I want it in there. I'm still president of this firm. I'm still the boss and I have enough stock to prove that."

"It won't be worth so much when we lose Douglas Lumber," Pete said softly.

Murch carefully avoided a change of expression. So the little man knew about Douglas Lumber.

Murch said evenly, "That's my worry. Yours is to help on this LeLane's pitch. You've been trying to mastermind it, and I haven't objected. You and Mike came up with some good ideas. I buy them. But I also want to see an intelligent pitch for a service fee arrangement. That's where you stopped playing ball."

"That's right, Murch. I don't agree. And that's why it isn't in that booklet."

"It is now," said Murch. "I wrote it in last night. And I'm going to talk about it during the presentation."

"We're dead if you do!" Pete replaced his glasses with a vicious gesture.

"I think not," said Murch. "I think Old Man Gortzein might like it. He might figure he wasn't getting enough for his money from the agency he's firing. With the service fee everyone comes out pretty well."

"It cuts down our take. We wouldn't—"

"We wouldn't be tempted to load a schedule, or go hog-wild on production costs, or—"

"I say it would be a mistake to talk it."

"I say not."

The men glared at one another, motionless, breathing a little hard. Finally Pete jabbed his glasses back on again, and then in a small burst of energy lit a cigarette, snapping his lighter viciously. "Okay. Let's put it to a vote in the agency," he said.

Murch shook his head. "In a creative session I'll welcome everyone's ideas—that's what an ad agency lives on. But on financial policies we don't go the committee route. Is that clear?"

"You're making yourself clear about a lot of things."

"I hope so."

Lanham looked as if he was about to erupt in another burst of anger, and took off his glasses again. After a moment he replaced them, smoked nervously for a few seconds, staring into Murch's face. Murch sat quietly, smiling at the smaller man, waiting.

"You usually have a choice," Pete said. "If you don't like it, you can shut up and take it—or you can get out. This isn't worth getting out about. I'll go along with you. I don't agree. I think it's wrong. But I'll admit it has worked here and there. It might— just *might*, in my opinion—work here."

"That's the way I wrote it into the pitch. Just a suggestion."

"Okay," Pete nodded. "Anything else?"

"Andes will be here this afternoon. Do you think we're ready?"

"Enough to start," Pete said. Apparently he had dismissed his anger as quickly as he had entertained it.

Murch got out the draft of the booklet from a brief case, glanced through it briefly, and handed it to the smaller man.

Pete took it and went out. Murch looked at the empty doorway and shook his head. He opened a drawer and searched for aspirin. The pain was starting in the back of his neck.

Diana Colton and Rick Andes walked up from the beach late in the morning. They had sunned since about nine o'clock, and Andes planned to leave during the noon hour for Douglas City for his first meeting at the agency.

Rick frowned. "I'm still not certain I like it."

"Because I'm Murch's wife?" she inquired sweetly. "I've told you not to worry about that. It's in name only. You're not taking anything that belongs to him. I belong to no one. Not even you, Rick. But I am willing and happy to give myself as I wish."

Andes smiled ruefully. "Basically I'm a very simple guy when it comes to what's between men and women. And if a man can't look after what he has, maybe he deserves to lose it. And evidently something's missing between you two. That's none of my business. As for you and me, I want you and it's good between us. That's that."

"So what bothers you?" she asked.

"This other bit—doing the pitch for the agency. That's a direct relationship between Murch and me. Maybe I just don't like the idea of working for a man while I'm sleeping with his wife."

"Only you're wrong. For all intents and purposes, my relationship with Murch is practically that of ex-wife. I've told you the marriage doesn't exist in essence, only in name."

"You're good with words."

"Is that the only way I'm good?" she asked coyly.

His alert, dark-brown, athlete's eyes traveled quickly over the length of her exposed body, almost seeing through the halter that outlined her breasts.

"No. You're good in other ways," he said. "Damned good. Don't ever sell yourself short."

She laughed, pleasure showing in a slight blush. Suddenly she was very conscious of her body, and she felt the stirring of desire. She looked at his brown shoulders, the breadth of his chest, the compact, solid swing of his torso, of hips and legs.

"I'm glad I please you," she said brazenly. "I'd like to please you now—*right* now. As soon as we get to the apartment."

"You know how to talk about it," he said. "I like that, too. You're sure as hell a man's woman. A man like me."

"I've never known a man like you before. You take care of me. You're good for me. Maybe I show it when I'm bedded down with you. Do I?"

"Yes," he said simply …

"Let's hurry. We'll have time before you leave."

In the apartment she locked the door and pulled down the shades. They showered together, hurriedly. He carried her to the bed, and she was as eager as he.

The union was consummated quickly, forcefully, vigorously. She gasped in the relentless but welcome slight hurt of reception and then she moaned and tears came to her eyes as she breathed the endearments of love-making, and finally short, brazen words that she never uttered elsewhere, nor had ever used before.

She reveled in her earthiness and vulgarity and female involvement that went beyond the quiet depths of gentle passion to a bitchiness of scratching, biting, threshing abandon. And finally he held her so close with his strength and male vigor that her moan became a low, plaintive keen of anguish in her intense pleasure and deliverance.

They rested, exhausted for the moment. He sprawled upon his back, smiling and shaking his head slightly.

"Good God, but you *are* a woman!" he said.

"For you," she said. "Only for you. Now do you understand? Don't worry about anything else. I give myself where I choose, and as much of me as I choose. And now you should know it's for you."

He shook his head again and rolled over. "Is my back bleeding? You scratched."

She raised herself on one elbow and giggled a little as her fingers gently traced long scratches down his back. "The skin is broken," she admitted. She pressed against him, her breasts against his back, her hands sliding over his shoulders.

"Again?" he asked.

"Can you?"

"After a little. But I have to leave within an hour."

"Maybe I can help," she murmured. Her mouth played along his shoulder muscles and she moved suggestively.

He rolled to his back again and held her against him. "Maybe you *could* help," he admitted. "Maybe you just could, you sweet-laying bitch!"

"Is that how you think of me?"

"So?"

"I like it. I like it that way. I'll show you again. I'll be a bitch and sweet-lay my man!"

He chuckled, and with the competent ease and strength of a graceful athlete he maneuvered her body to accept the reawakened demands of his desires.

In Murch's office, Bill Rhodes finished reading aloud the last of the presentation and sat back and looked at the others. Murch, Pete, Mike, Lorrie and Linda all nodded as if on cue.

"You've done one hell of a job," Murch said. "I like all of it." He looked around. "Bill's copy, the art and visuals Mike and Lorrie have dreamed up, and all to be sparked by a guy like

Andes—I don't see how we can miss!" He looked at Linda. "And you, Linda—Bill said you can write fashion copy. Now we all know it."

Linda blushed.

Pete said, "Mike and I *thought* we had a real one with this idea! Now we're certain.'

Bill hid a small smile as Pete made his bid for credit. He and Lorrie exchanged knowing glances. Linda still watched Murch, and the blush lingered. She valued his praise highly and already she was dreaming a short, quick dream about a Madison Avenue office and a slightly older, more mature, highly salaried career girl, Linda Smith, at a desk there.

Mike was almost preening himself in satisfaction.

Murch grinned. "Now that we know we're good, let's break for lunch. Andes will be here this afternoon."

The girl at the switchboard stopped Bill as they filed past her.

"You had a call, Bill. A woman. She gave me a hotel phone number and a suite. No name. She wants you to call at once."

Bill thanked her and went to his office. Instinctively he knew, and he tried to stop the fluttering in the pit of his stomach as he dialed and asked for the suite. He knew the voice at once.

"It's Bill," he said quietly. "Are you out here for the pitch, Kate?"

"Of course!" she said. "And I thought we might have lunch. Here at the hotel."

"I didn't think you'd come," he said.

"Or did you *hope* I wouldn't?" she asked, a small laugh in her voice.

Bill smiled. There was no point in trying to evade anything, cloak anything, or make small talk with Kate. They knew one another too well. At least, that was one thing you got out of marriage, even if you didn't get permanence.

"I'll be there in about ten minutes," he told her. "Downstairs, or do you want me to come up?"

"Come up. I'm still unpacking. I'll have martinis waiting."

They broke the connection. Bill lit a cigarette and drew the smoke deep into his lungs. He went to a window and looked down into the street, not seeing the scene, his eyes clouded in thought, his smile becoming grim. Finally he turned and left the agency.

Outside, the heat was intense under a noon sun. He decided to walk the short distance to the hotel. He wanted to think.

It was cool in the hotel. Kate Rhodes opened the door to his quiet knock and held out a drink for him. She closed the door behind him as he came in and stepped back to look at him.

"It hasn't been that long." He smiled at her scrutiny. "Only a few days ago in New York."

"Oh, I'm just sizing up an adversary," she told him. "And looking at you in your own habitat. People somehow change color—personality color, that is—when they visit New York. Sometimes the change is permanent, or it stays until they leave. Bill, you age well. Do you know that? I didn't tell you in New York, but I thought it."

"You're hardly a decrepit wreck yourself, lady," he said. He sipped at his drink and took the same liberty of sizing her up as she had taken with him. "One thing—you don't spread. And I don't think it's a girdle."

"Bill ... you *are* sweet!" she said.

"Sexy-looking, too," he said with a feigned look of lewdness.

"I *am* sexy, sort of! Don't you remember?"

Bill drank the rest of his martini, his fingers tightening slightly around the stem of the glass. It had begun as light badinage—light words between a divorced pair who had remained dear friends—but the words stirred memories. He remembered only too well how sex had been with them; it probably had been the only good thing about the marriage at the time. He knew the contours of her body, the movements, the demands, intensities and skills.

"Don't think about it, Bill," she urged quietly. She had guessed his thoughts. "It doesn't do any good. But if it helps any, I'll confess that I think about it sometimes, and I'll admit that *that* wasn't part of the divorce."

"I know," he said simply. "So we'll dismiss it lightly now. Ready for lunch?"

She finished her drink and nodded. They left the suite and went down to the dimly lit refuge of the highly touted hotel cocktail and luncheon room. They ordered solid, filling roast beef, and another drink while they waited.

"Bill," she said candidly, "we know you folks are pitching LeLane's. You know that we are. CWC intends to get the account. We're rough, tough, smart, and ready for this one. I just want you to know that I'm out here to fight you, but that it isn't personal between you and me."

"Naturally," Bill agreed.

"Don't look for any quarter, Bill. And I'll expect none from you."

"Can you tell me one thing, Kate? Why does CWC want the account? It's small to them."

"I shouldn't answer, Bill. We're friendly enemies, or whatever they call it these days. But I remember one very nice thing about you—you never reveal a confidence. So I know I can talk frankly to you."

"Want to tell me?"

"It doesn't make much difference. Knowing won't help you meet our competition, and it would only flatter LeLane's if you told them. We're spreading our wings into the fashion field. We want the LeLane's account because we think it's a firm that deserves to go to the top. It has everything to do it with—brains, facilities, energy, knowhow. It just hasn't had the proper agency to pave the way. That answer your question?"

"Yes. I thought as much. Anything you want *me* to tell *you?* Anything unclassified, that is?"

"Yes. I want to know if you ever miss me. If you—? Well, let's leave it at that."

Bill finished his second drink and his eyes locked with hers.

"Yes," he said simply. "It's still there. I'd like to get up, grab you by your beautiful hair, drag you upstairs, throw you on your divorcee bed and love hell out of you. That answer your question?"

"Completely," she said. "There are times when I think I was a damned fool to ever give you up, Bill Rhodes. Maybe that's why I instinctively kept your name."

He shrugged. He wasn't certain he believed her about the name. She never had liked her maiden name.

She saw his disbelief and for a second a flash of anger crossed her eyes and he saw it. She didn't like to be caught in deceit. She never had. She smiled quickly to cover the anger.

"Just what *are* you going to pitch to LeLane's?" she asked casually.

"Classified," he grinned. "But it was a nice try, Kate."

The first run-through of the presentation was a success.

They used the conference room, pushing back the long table and setting up easels, frames of corkboard, and other odds and ends of props for the selling effort.

While making introductions, Murch had experienced a moment of inquisitiveness as he introduced Mike to the ex-football star. He remembered the hint Lorrie had dropped about Mike's interest in Andes, and instinctively he watched for some small, overt gesture that would betray Mike.

There had been none. Actually, Mike's own well-proportioned body, poise, and general appearance oddly matched that of the athlete's. As the two men acknowledged the introduction with smiles and a hard handshake, it occurred to Murch that they looked like two opposing football coaches shaking hands before a bowl game. Certainly Mike showed no indications of the deviation of which he might be a victim.

Later, however, as the two men went to work on the various segments of the rehearsal, Murch noticed that Mike put his hands on Rick Andes at every opportunity; on an arm, a shoulder, against his side.

If the television star was aware of Mike's physical contacts, he displayed no signs of it. Murch surmised that Mike's very masculine appearance possibly would preclude any suspicion upon the part of Andes, and he was very certain that any masculine advances to the ex-football player would be strongly, if not violently, repulsed. He had heard now and then of Rick's success with women, and his proclivity to them.

But as the afternoon wore on, a strange excitement seemed to build in Mike, and Murch was certain that not all of it was from the intensity of the work. Mike's eyes sought Andes more frequently, his talk was addressed more specifically to the big man, his attention was centered upon him.

Once Murch found Lorrie looking at him with a worried frown, and he knew that she, too, had seen the strange build-up of excitement in her husband.

It was almost five o'clock when they finished for the day. They left the smoke-filled conference hall and walked down the hallway toward their various offices. Mike talked animatedly with Rick Andes. Pete already was in his office using a telephone. Murch found himself walking beside Lorrie.

"I'm worried," she said frankly in a low voice.

"Mike?" he asked.

"You noticed."

"Maybe it doesn't mean anything—just enthusiasm at seeing someone do a good job. And Andes *is* good."

"Excellent," she said. "I hope you're right."

Ahead of them Andes stopped and waited.

"When do we have another practice session?" he asked.

"Day after tomorrow?"

"Okay. I'll be in. Any message for your wife?"

"You might tell her about our session. She'll be interested."

"Fine." Andes nodded briskly and left.

"He really punches his lines," Murch said approvingly. "It's one hell of a good pitch, Lorrie.'

Mike, who stood in the doorway, looked after the departing man. "He's marvelous," Mike said softly. "Simply marvelous!" He seemed almost unaware that anyone else was near him.

Lorrie looked quickly at Murch, and neither of them smiled.

"That man is truly marvelous!" Mike said again. He turned and went briskly into his office.

"Oh, Murch ..." Lorrie said in a small, worried voice.

"Yes, I know," Murch said. "But let's wait. Maybe it will die out."

"I'm afraid."

Looking into her face, Murch knew that she truly was.

"We'll watch it closely," he said. "Maybe I can do something if it gets bad."

"I doubt it," Lorrie said. "Maybe this is the time ..."

CHAPTER SEVEN

D URING THE NEXT TWO DAYS Bill, Mike and Murch worked overtime, not only on the pitch, but to keep up the routine work for their regular clients.

One of their local accounts, an automobile dealer, decided to stage a fast promotion. It was Pete's account, and he called a creative session with Murch and the two department heads.

The dealer bought the campaign. Bill and Linda hurriedly wrote a full series of television and radio spots.

Meanwhile, Murch kept a close watch on Douglas Lumber. Nothing seemed to be happening until Murch sent proofs on hardboard ads for shelter magazines to the lumber firm. The advertising manager called and asked him to cancel the ads.

"What does that mean?" Murch asked apprehensively.

"Maybe next month," the advertising man said. "Can you make the switch?"

"I don't know," Murch said. "I can cancel, of course. Only I think you may be making a mistake. These ads hit at a good time. Good weather will be over and the do-it-yourself market will be active. Hardboard is one of your biggest sellers to that market."

"Murch, you don't have to tell me," the advertising manager said, a little testily.

"Just want to do a good job for you," Murch said. He had pressed a little too hard in his effort to get information. But the cancellation could mean that the firm didn't expect to be in business by the time the ads would have appeared. Or it could mean that they simply wanted to cut advertising expenditures. Whatever the reason, obviously Murch was not going to learn at once.

Work on the LeLane's presentation took all of Lorrie's time and most of Mike's. Rick Andes came in several times.

One afternoon, shortly after lunch, Pete came into Murch's office and closed the door, a signal that he wanted a conference.

"Walt Mickels let something slip," he said.

"What?"

"Bill's ex-wife is making a big play for Mickels and Old Man Gortzein. What's more, she's scoring."

"Kate? Well, she's quite a woman. You've seen her, haven't you?"

"Haven't we all? With Mickels or Gortzein. At lunch. At a bar with Mickels. Gortzein had her out to his place."

"Any ideas?"

"Bill's acting damned funny about it," Pete snapped. "Maybe he could soften her. He's seen her a couple of times. He admits that. I wanted him to find out what they intend to pitch, but he balks. Sometimes I don't know about Bill."

"Know what?"

"Where his loyalties are. What do you think?"

"I think it's none of our damned business what Bill chooses to do about his ex-wife. If he said no, that's it."

"For Christ's sake! You, too? What do you think business is—a game of touch football among friends? Hell, it's for keeps. Anything goes."

"We don't see alike, Pete. Leave Bill out of it as far as Kate Rhodes is concerned. Anyhow, she wouldn't tell him anything. She's on the first team back East. Be honest—she's forgotten more about her side of the business than some of us will ever learn. For my money she's the only hurdle we have, and I don't know how to get over it."

"I damned well do!" Pete said. "Fight fire with fire. Walt goes for Linda. She could be a big help to the agency right now. She could influence Walt's vote one hell of a lot."

Murch's eyes narrowed. "Aren't you pushing?"

"I don't think so," Pete said evenly. "I'm not asking Linda to give her all—if she still has it to give. Just to keep him away from Kate Rhodes. She ought to go out to the plant more. I think Old Man Gortzein likes her, too."

"Knock it off, Pete."

"Jesus! You've got a dirty mind. I told you I don't want her to go to bed with them. She just has to be charming and intelligent. Besides, she's a damned good copywriter. That's something for us to sell."

"Her copywriting services, yes. Nothing else."

Pete shrugged. "Okay. But let me point out something. If she *wants* to date Walt, or even Old Man Gortzein, that's *her* business—as much as Kate is Bill's. We can't interfere with Linda's life. Right?"

"Obviously," Murch said, not liking the logic behind the small man's statement, but recognizing it.

"Then there's no problem," Pete said.

Murch scowled as he watched Pete leave his office. He didn't trust his business partner.

A few moments later when he walked out of his office he was just in time to see Pete and Linda leave the agency.

"Where are they going?" he asked Helen.

The capable secretary looked up at him wisely. "Out to LeLane's. He was telling her he wants her to get to know Walter Mickels and Mr. Gortzein better. And I don't know if he meant as a copywriter or as a female. Okay, bossman?"

He nodded, smiling at her flipness, yet knowing that out of loyalty to him she was worried about Pete and Linda.

He returned to his office and had been there only a few moments when Rick Andes came in.

"Hi, Murch. Had some business at the station. Thought I'd stop by. Anything new on the pitch?"

"Nothing. Have you seen Diana?"

"Occasionally. She spends a lot of time on the beach."

"She always did," Murch said. "She likes sun."

Rick closed the door and sat in the chair beside Murch's desk. "Mind if we talk?" he asked.

"Something special?"

Rick brought out cigarettes. Murch flicked a lighter for them.

"This isn't something I *want* to talk about," Rick said. "And if I'm reading the signals wrong, tell me. And that'll be that. But I want to know."

Murch smoked quietly, oddly apprehensive. "Something bothering you?" he asked, when the silence became a little long.

"Yeah," Rick said, and grinned crookedly. "I was just trying to frame the question. Guess the best way is short and sweet. Tell me—what makes with your boy Mike?"

Murch felt a cold knot settle in the pit of his stomach. "I don't understand."

Rick looked closely into his face and then relaxed and inhaled deeply. "I think you do, Murch. Don't worry. I can handle things. I won't slug anyone. Only the guy *is* a little on the queer side. The guy's a homo, isn't he?"

"Has he made passes at you?" Murch asked.

"Are you kidding? He can't keep his hands off me. He looks at me like a high-school fullback drooling over some chick he wants to lay."

"Look, Rick, I don't know what to say."

"At least you're not denying it. I just wanted to be a little more certain—to be sure you know what's going on. Now I'm sure. Some guys would probably hang a fist on his jaw, but I won't. If he annoys me enough, I'll just tell him to look somewhere else. There'll be no trouble unless he brings it on. Check?"

"I'm sorry this had to happen, Rick."

"Hell, it's not your fault. So the guy's queer. He's still a hell of a good artist for you, isn't he?"

"One of the best."

"So I'm shocked? Look, Murch—TV has a few of them, too. Some top talent included. It's just that I don't like them. If it gets too much I'll cool your boy—but not with fists. Just politely and nicely, but it might break his little heart, and he might flip. I don't want you blaming me."

"I don't think it'll get that far," Murch said. "I don't think he's overt."

"Then we've nothing to worry about. I'll be on my way. Any message for Diana?"

"Tell her to have a good time," Murch said. "And, Rick— thanks for talking it over with me."

"Sure. You know … sometimes I feel sorry for a guy like that. In some ways he's okay—talent-wise. Too bad he hasn't got the rest of it in the right place."

The big man had been gone only a few moments when Mike came in.

"Did I hear Rick's voice?" the artist asked.

"He just left."

A look of disappointment crossed Mike's face. "I do wish he'd stopped in to see me. Are you certain he's gone?"

"He said he was returning to the beach at once."

"He could have stopped," Mike said, now peevish.

"Something important?" Murch asked, watching the other man's face and thinking about what Rick had just talked about.

"Well, we *are* trying to prepare a presentation, Murch!" Mike said impatiently. "I have to work very closely with Rick."

"He'll be back in a day or so," Murch said.

Mike almost flounced out and walked quickly down the hallway. Out of curiosity Murch went to the door. The artist said something to the switchboard girl and left the agency, obviously after Rick.

Even as Murch stood in the doorway, Lorrie came out of her office and caught a glimpse of her husband leaving. For a few seconds she stood motionless, then she turned and looked at Murch. She shrugged.

Murch joined her in the art department. Lorrie stood at a window and pensively gazed down into the street.

Murch said, "He didn't like it because Rick was here and didn't stop in to see him."

She nodded without comment.

"I may as well tell you," Murch continued. "Rick knows about Mike. That's why he stopped by."

Lorrie looked at him quickly, a shadow of fear clouding her face.

"Murch! He won't do anything? I mean, he's big and a football player and—well, men like that are so masculine and—"

"No violence. As a matter of fact, he's pretty sensible and understanding. He doesn't like it, but he'll only tell Mike off if it goes too far."

"That could be almost as bad as hitting him," Lorrie said. She shook her head impatiently. "Don't misunderstand me, Murch. I'm not particularly defending Mike, only ... well, he's sick. I guess I'm protective. He's almost like a child."

"Not quite," Murch said evenly.

She looked startled by his words and the tone of his voice.

"Oh …" she said. "Yes. You're right."

"We'll just have to ride it out. Meanwhile, show me what you've got on the proposed campaigns."

They went over the art work she had done. It was good—she had a feel for fashion and expression.

Murch said, "I knew you were good, Lorrie, but never realized *how* good!"

"Thank you, Murch. I've a special interest in this job. I do so want you to get LeLane's."

A telephone rang and Lorrie answered. The conversation was brief. She hung up thoughtfully.

"Mike," she said. "He didn't catch up with Rick, and he's at a bar. He won't be home for dinner."

Murch's eyebrows went up in a silent question.

"I don't know," said Lorrie. "Sometimes he goes on a drunk. A solitary, brooding, almost vicious sort of thing."

"Have dinner with me," he said.

"I'd better work here tonight. We don't have much time left."

"I'm coming back, too."

"All right," she murmured. She looked tired. "But just dinner, Murch? And back here to work? Nothing to complicate things?"

"Of course." He knew what she meant. Sometimes you had to make a choice between emotions and work. You couldn't always afford the luxury of them together. "Just work," he said.

They labored until almost midnight. The presentation was taking form rapidly, but a great deal of work remained.

"It still needs polish," Murch told her as he drove her home.

"I have an idea," Lorrie said. "Remember I did some work for LeLane's. And I learned then that they worry about their collateral stuff. Hang-tags, the sales kits they give their salesmen, trade ads, mailers to the trade, showings, point-of-sale display stuff."

Murch looked at her, almost startled. She was right. They had concentrated too much on their experience, creative ability, facilities, and ideas for national campaigns. The collateral material was equally important.

"You're so damned right!" he exclaimed.

"I've worked up some collateral stuff. If you like I'll concentrate on more."

"I'm not even certain what we'll need," Murch admitted. "How much work will this take, Lorrie?"

"Some overtime. And I'll need some help from Bill and Linda."

"Mike?"

"He's not interested in this."

"All right—you go on the collateral."

They arrived at the McPherson house. It was dark and no car was in the garage.

"Mike's not home," Murch observed.

Lorrie bit her lower lip worriedly. "I hope he's all right."

"Do you want me to come in?"

She looked at him directly. "You'd better not, Murch. Let's still keep things separate."

He nodded. "See you in the morning."

"Yes," she murmured. Almost before he realized what she had done, she leaned forward and kissed him gently and quickly on the lips. Then, before he could take her in his arms, she was out of the car and at her door, looking back and waving. He waited until lights went on before he drove away.

He wondered if he should go to town and make a search for Mike. The agency couldn't afford to have the art director on a protracted drunk right now. Too much was at stake. But he didn't know where he could find him.

Wearily he drove home. The house was hot in the summer night. He repeated the ritual of opening windows, checking the mail, and finally mixing a strong nightcap. He hoped it would make him sleep. The pace was beginning to tell on him.

The next morning he fought to awaken. A cold shower helped a little. He heated water, doubled a serving of instant coffee into a cup and drank the strong brew.

On the way to the office he stopped at a chain-store café for juice, ham, eggs, toast and coffee. He felt better after the more substantial breakfast.

He arrived at the office early again, and Bill was looking through the first mail. The copy chief tossed the envelopes on the receptionist's desk.

"I wonder if all agencies get as much junk mail," he said.

Murch grinned. "When we prepare it for a client, it's a direct mail campaign. When we get it from others, it's junk!"

"Yeah," Bill agreed. "Viewpoint is everything. Anything new?"

Murch rapidly filled him in on his conversation with Lorrie and the decision to do more collateral material.

"Lorrie's right," Bill said. "Sometimes I'm not so sure we should be pitching a fashion account."

"We could use a little more experience. But in Lorrie we have it, so we're lucky. Help her all you can, Bill."

"Harold's wife just phoned," Bill said. "She wants you to call her."

Murch frowned and dialed the home number of the third principal of the firm. Martha Simpson's voice answered. "Murch? I'm glad you called. I was just leaving for the hospital. Harold had another bad night."

"How serious?" Murch asked.

"It wasn't nearly as serious as the other. But I had a long talk with the doctor. He says Harold can't return to work for at least three months, and possibly longer."

"If that's what the doctor says, that's the way it is, Martha. Don't you worry, and tell Harold not to worry. I'm sure he'll be all right."

"That's what I told him. So did the doctor. He's fussing?"

"Tell him we'll take care of things here."

"I've already talked with Pete. When I couldn't get you. He said the same thing—for us not to worry."

"Tell Harold I'll try to see him today, although I may get hung up. And, Martha—call me if you need anything. Any time."

"Thanks, Murch. We're lucky to have people like you and Pete—"

"We're lucky to have Harold—and we want to keep him!"

They finished their conversation and he put down the telephone. Bill listened gravely to the news.

"Puts us in a spot," Bill said.

The telephone rang and Bill answered. "For you," he said. "It's Pete."

Murch answered.

Pete said, "Martha reach you yet? About Harold?"

"I just talked with her."

"I've been doing some thinking. With the way things are right now, I can take over the whole production chore. If necessary, we can hire some help later."

Murch frowned. He didn't like the turn of events. Pete knew production, but this would give him additional power in the agency—there seemed to be no other way out. They couldn't bring in a stranger, and he, Murch, was not a production man.

"We'll talk about it when you get in," Murch said.

"I'll be late. I'm meeting Linda out at LeLane's."

"You're not forgetting our talk, are you?"

"What does that crack mean?"

"You know what I'm talking about, Pete. Which way are you selling her?"

"Jesus! You and your suspicions. We're going to talk with some department heads—for copy slants. Okay?"

Murch put his hand over the mouthpiece and said to Bill: "Did you know Linda is meeting Pete out at LeLane's this morning?"

Bill shrugged. "It's getting to be a habit," he said "But she is turning out copy. Maybe it's all legitimate."

"Okay, I'll see you this afternoon," Murch said into the telephone.

He hung up again, and they walked down the hallway. Behind them the main door to the agency opened and two of the girls came in, followed by Mike and Lorrie. Mike looked as if he had a hangover. He went directly to his office without greeting the two men. Lorrie looked at them and shrugged. She followed her husband into the art department.

"And a happy good-morning to you, too!" Bill muttered.

Murch went to his office and waited. In ten minutes he heard Lorrie walk down the hallway and stop at his open doorway. He looked up and motioned her in. She entered, closed the door, and leaned back against it, as she had done once before. Again he rested one hand against the door and kissed her. She was receptive and came close to him. Then she pushed him back with a gentle hand.

"Have you a cigarette?" she asked.

He got out cigarettes. She sat in the chair by his desk.

"He didn't get home until after three this morning," she said. "Loaded?"

"He could hardly walk. I've never seen him like that. He wouldn't speak to me. This morning, either. I don't know …"

"We'll have to wait it out. Martha Simpson called. Harold won't be back for months. Pete wants to take over production."

"Is that a good idea?"

"No, but I can't handle it. Pete can. Actually, right now all I want is to get that damned pitch finished and pitched, and know whether or not we're going to have the account."

Lorrie nodded. They smoked in silence for a half moment and then Lorrie said quietly, "Mike says Douglas Lumber is in danger, Murch. He got it from Pete."

Murch smiled grimly. "There's no reason you shouldn't know, Lorrie. You're part of the team. Only I didn't think Pete would be passing out the information."

"How serious is it?"

"They just canceled ads in their shelter magazine schedule. It could be very serious."

"I'd better get back. I don't want Mike to think anything. Although I don't think he could care less. I'm really worried this time, Murch. He's never been quite like this. Have you seen the way he looks at Rick Andes?"

"I've seen. So has Rick. Maybe we're in trouble."

Pete arrived with Linda after lunch. The girl was excited and talkative. Murch could hear her chattering with Bill and then sounds of furious typing as she worked material into copy form. He went to Pete's office. The short, bespectacled man was busy at his desk. He looked up impatiently.

Murch closed the door. He said, "Let's check out a few things, Pete."

"Something troubling you?"

"Quite a few things—including this deal with Linda. She's a nice kid. Let's not dirty things."

"You're crazy. She's over twenty-one. She leads her own life. Since when did you join the Salvation Army?"

"Don't push," Murch said softly. "You know what I mean."

Pete leaned back in his chair. "S-a-a-y … *you're* not interested in her, are you, Murch?"

For a second Murch felt like taking the smaller man by the coat lapels and shaking him. He fought down the anger. "You're out of bounds now," he said.

"Am I? She's got a yen for you, Murch. Or didn't you notice?"

"You're crazy."

Pete shrugged. "Maybe I'd be doing you a favor if I got her interested in someone else. Then we wouldn't be having any office incidents. They're messy sometimes."

"Knock it off. I mean it."

As quickly as he put the bantering edge to his voice, Pete Lanham dropped it for a metallic hardness. "All right, let's deal 'em face up. What's biting you? The production department? That it?"

"Maybe," Murch snapped. "That's Harold's job—he still owns part of this agency, and we're going to protect his job for him. Is that clear?"

"For God's sake! You act like I'm trying to ace Harold out of the agency by taking over his department!"

"I'm just stating facts," Murch said.

"What makes with you, anyhow, Murch? You think I'm trying to pull a fast one? That I hate your guts?"

"Well?" Murch challenged.

Pete Lanham looked at him silently for a moment and then shoved his glasses firmly into place. "All right," he said. "We'll talk about it. You remember the drug account?"

Murch's eyes widened a little and suddenly he did understand some of the conflict between them.

"That's history," Murch said. "So you made a mistake. You took on a crummy, fast-buck drug outfit—the Federal people got on them for misrepresentation and we lost a few thousand. I blew my top. It's ancient history now."

"Not that ancient, Murch. I still resent things you said. And no apologies afterwards."

"None were due. What do you want to do about it?"

"Just get it out in the open. We can still operate all right. We all have a place in this agency. But I want you to know how it is."

"Maybe you'd better get out if that's the way you feel."

"You forget that I own some of the shop, too. Have *you* thought about leaving?"

"Are you crazy?"

"So stay. Only let's remember that I'm largely responsible for what may come out of LeLane's pitch. I've built it up. You're on the verge of losing Douglas Lumber, and when you do, *my* accounts will be billing *half as much again* as yours. And Harold never did bill any accounts. He contributes production knowledge—and that's all. So that's how it stands."

"Except for a few other things," said Murch. "First, with my stock I still control the agency while Harold backs me—which he will. Second, until, and if, we lose Douglas Lumber, I control most of the billing. Third, the invitation from LeLane's to make a presentation came to the agency—not to you, nor to me—but to the *agency*. You happened to know Mickels, so you waded in. But I'm still running things, including the presentation."

"You're taking a lot for granted, Murch."

"I'm not finished. Let's have a showdown right now. *I'm* not getting out. Now if *you* want out, say so."

Pete Lanham shook his head. "And walk out when we have a chance to get LeLane's? No, thanks. I'm staying. And let's face one other thing—if we get it, I think Mickels and Gortzein will specify *me* as account executive. It will be *my* account. Because they know I'm originating the presentation."

"What do you want, Pete? What are you after?"

"Lelane's. I'll take it from there. Believe me, I will."

Murch forced a tight smile and left the office. Pete worried him more than he wanted to admit, and he realized now that the small man had burned under the criticism on the disastrous drug account. Pete Lanham hated criticism. He hated to be wrong. And he was ambitious and ruthless in his own, vicious way.

Helen Vaughan stopped him. "There was a call for you," she said. "Mrs. Simpson."

"It isn't Harold?" Murch snapped in sudden fear. He was fond of the production man. They had worked together for years.

"I don't think so," Helen said. "She said it's important, but it can wait if you're too busy. She's at home."

He dialed from his office. Martha Simpson answered.

"What's wrong, Martha? Is Harold all right?"

"It isn't Harold, Murch. It's something else. I don't know what to think."

"About what?"

"I talked with Pete this morning—as you know. And not long ago he called and asked about Harold, and then he said something rather odd."

"Yes?"

"He said if Harold decides to retire, he wants to buy Harold's stock in the agency—and he asked me to tell Harold."

"I see ..." Murch said thoughtfully. "What did you tell him, Martha?"

"I said that probably would be an agency decision. I told him Harold hadn't talked about retiring, and that the doctor had asked me not to talk business with him. We sort of left it at that. I thought I'd better tell you, Murch."

"Did he ask you not to mention it to me?"

"Frankly, he did. But I didn't promise anything. I hope I didn't—"

"It's all right, Martha," Murch interrupted. "And thanks for telling me. If Harold ever wants out, we'll all talk it over and see that the best deal possible is made for him."

"Thanks, Murch," she said. "I feel better for telling you."

After the conversation he was tempted to confront Pete with the attempt to buy out Harold Simpson, but he decided against it. The effort had accomplished nothing, and the feeling already was too tense. The main thing at the moment was to get the presentation ready.

He went into the art department. Lorrie and Mike were hard at work. Murch inspected some of the collateral material Lorrie had roughed out. It looked good. Mike graciously complimented her, but his thoughts seemed to be elsewhere. When Murch glanced at the artist's drawing board, he saw nothing but meaningless doodles. Some looked like the outlines of a man, and the man looked vaguely like Rick Andes.

"Trying to get some ideas," Mike said lamely. "I've got a king-size hangover."

"Why don't you go home?" Murch suggested "Take a break."

"Think I will," Mike said. "Do you mind, Lorrie?"

She shook her head. "I'm going to work tonight. Will you be here, Murch? I'm nervous about being here alone at night."

"I'll be here," he assured her.

Helen Vaughan came into the room.

"It's your day for telephone calls, boss-man," she announced.

He picked up a telephone and the switchboard girl put through the connection. The advertising director at Douglas Lumber identified himself.

"Murch," he said, "I might as well be blunt. It's happened. Douglas Lumber sold out this morning. We're going out of business as a firm and I.T.A. Plywood takes over. They have their own agency so—look, Murch, I hate like hell to do this to you, but this is it. I don't know what else to do. Unless I ask you for a job. I'll probably be out, too. I doubt if I.T.A. will take over many of the personnel—and certainly not the advertising department. Murch—I'm sorry …"

"It's all right," Murch said. "I've been expecting it. We can discuss it later. There just might be a spot here. Let's talk tomorrow. Okay?"

"Thanks, Murch. Christ, but those I. T. A. people are a bunch of cold sharks! The deal was announced this morning and they've begun firing already."

Mike had left during the phone call but Lorrie watched him apprehensively. When he dropped the telephone in its cradle she spoke. "Bad news," she said flatly. "It's in your eyes."

"We just lost Douglas Lumber."

"Oh, Murch … I'm sorry. With everything else—"

"Dinner with me tonight?" he asked, looking into her eyes.

She nodded silently.

"That's good," he said.

They both smiled, and he went out of the room and back to his office. He sat down and stared vacantly at his desk. After a few moments he sighed, picked up the phone and dialed an interoffice connection to Bill. When the copy chief answered Murch said, "You'd better come in here, Bill. I'm going to close the door and get out the client's bottle and pour us both a big slug of expensive Scotch."

"Celebration or dirge?"

"Dirge. We just lost Douglas Lumber."

CHAPTER EIGHT

MURCH ANNOUNCED THE LOSS of Douglas Lumber the following morning in a brief meeting in the conference room. Because most staff members were involved in one way or another, he had everyone at the meeting, and he broke the news quickly and succinctly.

Pete listened with a faint trace of a smile on his lips. Somehow he had obtained news of the break the night before and had greeted Murch with it the first thing in the morning. Murch had cut him short with the information that he was calling a staff meeting.

"So that's it," Murch concluded his announcement. "It's rough to take right now, but we have a chance of more than replacing the billing with LeLane's. We're actually in fair shape financially and we'll weather this storm. Of that I'm certain."

Some of the stenographers smiled nervously, not quite certain of the implications in the loss of a major account. Mike seemed to be almost indifferent, his thoughts elsewhere.

Following the meeting, Murch called a quick session of the creative people to check the status of the LeLane's presentation.

Murch and Lorrie had worked late the night before, and Mike had come down to take her home. He had been drinking and was almost indifferent to the work she had been doing. Murch had gone down into the street with them, relieved when Lorrie slid behind the wheel of their car.

After they had driven away, he had found a bar and sat drinking for an hour or so. He had left his car in the lot and had taken a taxi home to fall into bed, feeling the drinks in a numb, indifferent heaviness. He had slept soundly but had awakened with a slight hangover. Getting through the meeting had been difficult.

Now as the short creative session broke up, Murch found himself walking beside Pete. They went into Murch's office. Pete closed the door.

"Okay," Murch said. "So we've lost Douglas Lumber. What's on your mind, Pete?"

"An armistice until we finish the LeLane's pitch."

"I don't think you're in a spot to be setting down terms," Murch commented. "But I'll buy the armistice."

"Is Andes coming in today?"

"Yes. I had Helen call him. The collateral material will change our timing and some of the agenda."

Murch was relieved to call a halt to the mounting discord between them. There was too much to do.

He lunched with Bill and they drank too much. Tension was taking its toll. He took a long walk alone after lunch to clear his head. The summer heat was building again. He was glad to get back to the air-conditioned offices and some aspirin for his persistent headache.

He felt out-of-sorts and gruff when he went into the rehearsal meeting.

Andes came wearing slacks and sport shirt. He looked very brown and fit. Mike McPherson couldn't keep his eyes off the man.

They began the rehearsal and it became an intense work session. They used props. The film was ready and they ran segments of it. Graphs were put up and Rick made his scripted comments.

Financial and pertinent qualifying material was recited by Murch and Pete. They began work on the collateral section.

Mike bustled about arranging easels, graphs, art presentations and people. He fussed about where Rick should stand. His hands found their way to Rick's arms and shoulders at every opportunity.

Suddenly Rick dropped his script on a table and turned to face Mike, who had just tried to position himself at the proper place to use a pointer. Mike's hand still was on Rick's shoulder as the athlete turned. Rick swept the hand down with an impatient gesture, his eyes narrowing in anger.

"Mike—keep your goddamn hands off me," he said.

Mike stared at him, color draining from his cheeks and lips. "But, Rick—" he started to say.

"Skip it," Rick told him. He tried to smile, but it was a sad failure. His anger was too obvious. "Now you know, so skip it."

"I don't know what you—"

"Simply keep your hands off me. That's all."

Suddenly Mike turned and fled. Lorrie stood frozen, her eyes filled with tears. She looked at Murch and shook her head. The others in the room tried to cover their embarrassment. Rick looked around defiantly.

"I'm sorry," he said. "It's—well, I just don't like—oh, hell." He shrugged in the futility of trying to explain exactly what he meant, and what was so exactly obvious to everyone.

"Let's call it a day," Murch said. "There are some cuts to be made, but it shapes up pretty well. Rick, can you come in day after tomorrow?"

"I'll be here," Rick said. He left the room and Murch walked down the hallway with him. Rick said, "Look, Murch—I'm sorry as hell, but he'd been pawing me all afternoon and suddenly I'd had it.'

"I understand," Murch said, "and I'm sorry it happened. I don't know how we'll resolve this problem. He's a good artist and art director, but we can't tolerate this kind of thing."

"Maybe this was enough," Andes said. "Sometimes a guy like that only needs to be called once and it stops him."

"Maybe so," Murch said. "See you day after tomorrow, then?"

"Right."

"Diana okay? I haven't had time to call her."

"She looks great when I see her," Rick told him.

Murch walked to the door with Andes. Coming back he met Lorrie at the entrance to the art room. He glanced in. Mike was not there.

"I'm going home," Lorrie said. "I'd better be with him. He left a note saying he'd take a taxi. He left the car."

"Lorrie, I'm damned sorry—"

"You couldn't help it, Murch. Nor could Rick. It was certain to happen sooner or later. I just hope it doesn't—well, that it doesn't *do* anything to him."

Murch nodded. They said good night and he went to his office. Bill was waiting for him.

"So?" the copy chief said.

Murch shrugged. They both recognized the situation for what it was.

"Pete was unhappy," Bill said. He wants Mike on his side—wants all that talent. But the pansy bit scares hell out of him."

"Pete leave?"

"Yeah. He took Linda with him. Said he'd buy her a drink."

"They're getting too damned friendly!" Murch said, suddenly irritated.

Bill looked at him reproachfully. "Don't snap at me, Murch. I'm just reporting. I don't think there's anything brewing between them, but I do know she's dating Walt Mickels. And so is Kate."

"I didn't mean to snap at you. I'm sorry," Murch said. He pulled out a filing drawer and took out the client's bottle of Scotch. It was almost empty. He managed two drinks in water glasses and dropped the empty bottle in a basket.

"You're not drinking too much of this stuff?" Bill asked.

"For medicinal purposes only," Murch assured him. "Frayed nerves."

"Yeah. You look a little drawn and quartered."

They finished their drinks and ate at a nearby cafe. Later, as Murch returned to work, a shapely young girl walked in front of him, revealingly dressed in a tight summer skirt.

He watched the twitching sway of the girl, the very feminine walk, and suddenly realized that his observation was completely sexless and indifferent.

Maybe there is something in this sublimation bit, he told himself. *Maybe work* can *take the place of sex—but I doubt it!*

He grinned and crossed the street to a liquor store. He needed to replace the client's bottle in his file drawer. He bought two. He knew he'd open one before the night was over.

The switchboard girl had left a night connection to his office. Shortly after ten o'clock the telephone rang and he answered the call.

"Murch? I'm so glad you're there," Lorrie said. She sounded frightened. "Mike has been arrested."

"Arrested! What happened?"

"It's awfully sordid, Murch. We had dinner and he was restless and terribly moody. He'd been drinking. He wouldn't talk with me. Shortly after eight he said he was going out for a walk. I watched him walk as far as the corner and then I saw him take a bus. I began to worry. It isn't like him to use the bus. Then just a few moments ago he called from the police station. He was sort of incoherent about it all and finally a desk sergeant talked with me and I found out."

"What happened?"

"A vice detective arrested him in that park where the homo-sexuals hang out—the one that's always in the papers. The detective said that Mike accosted him on a park bench and made overt homosexual advances."

"You have your car there?"

"Yes."

"I'll meet you in front of the building."

She was there almost as soon as he had locked the office and roused the night man to take him down.

"Straight to the police station," he told her.

"I don't know what to do, Murch. This is so terrible—so alien to anything I know about."

"Don't worry. Things can be handled."

They parked near the police station and went into the building. It smelled of strong disinfectant. They studied the directory board, and finally Murch went to a young officer at a window labelled INFORMATION.

The young officer directed the couple to a room down a hallway. There a gray-haired officer in uniform listened to them. He looked sympathetically at Lorrie, and when he glanced at Murch's business card he was friendly and respectful.

"You understand, Mr. Colton—Mrs. McPherson—we have no other choice. The arresting officer was only doing his job."

"We can arrange for bail?" Murch asked.

"Certainly."

"Officer—there couldn't be as mistake?" Lorrie asked in a small voice.

The officer shook his head. "I'm sorry, Mrs. McPherson. Your husband has admitted the charge."

"What do we do?" she asked.

Murch said, "I'll post bail for him. We'll have our company attorney on it in the morning. Maybe we can arrange some psychiatric aid."

A half-hour later Mike accompanied them to the sidewalk. He appeared to be in a daze. They tried to talk with him, but he shook his head impatiently. At the car he walked quickly around to the driver's side and slid behind the wheel.

Murch started to open a door for Lorrie and himself, but Mike reached quickly across and snapped down the locking button. He rolled down the window an inch.

"No," he said. "I'm sorry. I appreciate what you've done. Both of you. But I can't face up to this. Not yet. I have to get away from here for a day or so."

"Please, Mike!" Lorrie cried. "Don't. It isn't as bad as you—"

"I'm going down to the beach where I can think," Mike said.

He started the car and drove away, leaving Murch and Lorrie on the sidewalk.

"Maybe he's right," Murch finally said. "It may be better for him to be alone and think it out."

Lorrie nodded and wiped a tear from a cheek, then looked up at him and tried to smile.

"Murch—I think I need a good, strong drink."

"There's a place down the street."

They sat at the bar in a small cocktail lounge and talked about Mike, the agency, what had happened. The drinks were potent and they relaxed. After a while they talked about themselves.

"I'll take you home," he finally said. "My car's in the lot. We'll taxi there."

In his car she sat close. He could feel her body warmth.

"I don't want to go home, Murch," she said. "It's almost as if someone had died. I don't want to be alone."

"Want me to stay awhile with you? I can come in for a drink."

"I don't want to be around anything that's Mike's tonight. I know he's sick, but there's something unclean and unnatural about this whole thing and I want to be clean and natural—do I make sense?"

"We could go to my place?"

"No. I'd be thinking about Diana. You and Diana there."

They rode in silence and suddenly he turned the car and drove toward a freeway. Neither spoke. Lorrie leaned forward and turned on the radio. She found a station broadcasting classical music. They listened to a Bruckner symphony. The music was powerful and stirring.

He turned into a luxurious motel on the edge of the next town. Lorrie didn't speak. She seemed to be absorbed by the music. He registered and came out with a key. The unit was at the far end of the drive. It was impeccably furnished. There were soft lights and a sprawling bed. The drapes were heavy. A television was silent, and there was a built-in radio. Murch turned on the radio and found the broadcast they had been hearing.

Now they stood in the center of the large room, in soft light, surrounded by music, and the door closed and locked so that they were completely in retreat from the world.

They looked at one another, smiling. He took her into his arms and they kissed, gently, and almost in tentative exploration. Then he held her away.

"You're sure?"

"Yes, Murch. I'm very sure."

She showered and he turned out the lights and waited while he listened to the music. She came out, a large bath towel wrapped around her as a sarong. She was willowy and graceful in the faint light that came through the dawn drapes.

He had pulled down the spread and covers on the bed. The sheets were white and receptive.

"I'll only be a few moments," he said.

The shower was needle sharp and he finished with cold water, toweled briskly, and then tied a fresh towel around his waist and came out into the room.

Lorrie waited for him on the bed, a sheet over her. The towel was draped on a chair. She had left on a small lamp by the radio.

"Do you mind the light, darling?" she asked. "The dark is too much as if we're ashamed. It's too furtive. I don't want to feel that way about us."

He walked to the side of the bed and looked down at her. The streak of gray in her hair suddenly was exciting. The softness and fullness of her lips seemed accentuated. Her smile was that of another woman; a welcoming, anticipating smile.

"You're beautiful," he said.

She shut her eyes and waited, the sheet pulled up to her chin, the contours of her breasts obvious and indiscreet beneath the linen. He reached down, almost breathlessly, and gently pulled the sheet down and away until it draped over the foot of the bed.

"So beautiful, Lorrie—more than I knew, more than I could ever realize …"

Carefully he bent to kiss her. His mouth tasted her lips, her woman's shoulders, her breasts, and she gasped and her hands sought him although her eyes stayed tightly shut.

He was beside her, then over her, and they moved and found their comfort, and she whispered, "Be gentle, Murch. It's been so long. This hasn't been between Mike and me … you know that … oh, yes, like that … gently, and … oh, Murch! … please! … oh, yes … yes … !"

They slept briefly and awoke.

"I love you," he told her. "I truly love you. It's never been like this."

"Never, never, never, Murch. Oh, never like this. So good for me—for us. Was I good for you, my darling?"

"There are no words for it."

"There must be, darling. Through all the centuries. How many words for it? We just can't be the only ones."

"We might have never known, though. We might have lived and died without knowing."

She laughed softly. "We talk lovers' talk, darling. Such a sweet language. Do all lovers say the same things, feel the same things, know the same things? They must. None of us is different enough from the other. Only I didn't know it before. Truly not like this. Murch, do I say it well?"

"Better than I, Lorrie. All I know is your beauty and you and everything that it is now—and never was before."

"We try so hard to say a simple thing: that we were together and it was good; that you had me, and it was good."

He reached for her and she moved willingly against him. They made love slowly and in a sweet rhythm of awareness until it was crested again in a demanding and sought-for violence.

This time they fell into sound sleep and it was gray with false dawn when Lorrie awakened him.

"Murch ... please ... wake up ..."

He was instantly awake and fully cognizant of where he was. He put an arm about her and drew her close and kissed her cheek.

"It's all right," he said.

"No, I don't mean that. Not us. What we have is ours now. Nothing can ever change that. It's not that. It's something about Mike."

"What?"

"Twice he's taken overdoses of sleeping pills. Twice he's tried to kill himself. Last night I didn't think. I just awakened thinking about it and now I'm frightened."

He raised himself on an elbow and looked down into her face. She regarded him with serious eyes.

"No, Murch," she said. "Not that kind of love for him. Just worry for him because he's so miserably sick. And he might do it now. It was such a shock to him last night."

"Lorrie, I don't believe he would—I mean ..."

She shook her head. "He might, Murch. If he did I'd hate myself for the rest of my life. I'd hate us. It hasn't anything to do with my marriage. That doesn't really exist. It's because he's a person, a human being, and I've had to look after him for so long. I couldn't stand having his death on my conscience simply because I didn't try to stop him."

"Do you think we should try to find him?"

"Yes, Murch. Please? Will you understand? *He* could never come between us now, Murch. But his *death* could. And I'm frightened. The doctors barely saved him the last time."

"We'll leave at once, darling."

The beach town was still asleep in the gray dawn when they arrived. It was the same town where Diana and Rick Andes were staying. Agency and media people usually selected it, and Lorrie was certain that Mike would come there.

"Any idea where we should look?" Murch asked.

"We've stayed at the apartments where you and Diana stay."

"We can try there. We can get Diana up and have coffee and she can help us. She may know where best to look. Only ... remember that Rick is here? Do you think that would keep Mike away?"

She looked at him thoughtfully. "I don't know, Murch. And do you think Diana is a good idea? I mean, the two of us—"

"Do we have a choice, Lorrie? If you're right about Mike we'd better find him. And we can't be down here looking without Diana knowing. She'll think it's sensible for me to bring you down to look for Mike. And it *is*. Meanwhile, what's ours—yours and mine—is simply ours, and we'll keep it that way. Later we can settle other questions."

"All right. I'll try to look as if nothing happened between us. Oh, Murch, now I'm embarrassed and—"

He squeezed her slim fingers. "Forget our own problem for now. Mike's life has to be thought of first."

"Yes," she said.

He stopped the car at the apartments where he and Diana had registered. He still had a key to their door. In his haste to leave for the city he had forgotten to leave it.

Quietly, they walked up a pathway. It had become light now. The roar of the breakers sounded especially loud in the early morning. The air was chilly. He unlocked the door and they went in.

"I'll go in and awaken her," he said, crossing to the bedroom. He opened it. Behind him, Lorrie saw him stop abruptly.

She looked beyond him to the double bed and saw Diana Colton's small, compact, nude body, and beside it the muscled, sinewy body of Rick Andes. He slept soundly, one arm thrown carelessly over the woman. A pillow was on the floor beside the bed. Diana lay in the sprawled, abandoned sleep of sexual satiation.

Lorrie forced her eyes away from the bed to Murch, almost fearfully. Who could ever know what a man might do in such circumstances? Even his own guilt, and hers, seemed somehow insignificant in the shock of discovering this obvious transgression.

For an instant she thought he would hurl himself into the room in a tremendous rage, and then he began slowly to relax.

He shook his head and turned. Gently, he pulled the door closed behind him and took Lorrie's hand to lead her from the apartment.

He didn't speak until they were in the car and he had driven away from the apartments and parked above the beach.

"Murch ..." she said hesitantly, not knowing exactly what to say. "I'm sorry."

"No," he said. "This only makes it easier. I think I've instinctively known all along. It's been over for a long time. At first, back there, I was almost crazy with anger—and then I wasn't. I realized my pride was hurt—that masculine pride of possession. Only she never was mine. And, equally important, I know now that I never was hers."

She watched him and waited. He lit a cigarette and sighed. "Okay," he said, "Let's look around. Maybe we can spot your car."

They found the car parked in front of a beachside curio shop that bore the name "Laddie's Shelter."

"Oh," Murch said cryptically. "Does he know Laddie?"

"Yes. They spend a great deal of time together when we're down here. Laddie's ... queer, isn't he?"

"The complete homo," Murch said.

"I ... I think I'm going to be sick, Murch. Honestly—"

He reached for her hands and squeezed them. "Swallow hard and breathe deeply," he told her. He opened a window. The sea air swept into the car. "Better?"

She nodded, but she was pale about the mouth.

"He found his own, I guess," she finally said.

They stared at the small apartment above the shop. Faintly they could hear music and then they heard two men laugh and one of the voices was Mike's.

Lorrie shuddered.

"Let's go back, Murch. Let's go home," she said.

CHAPTER NINE

THE NEXT FEW DAYS passed like a kaleidoscopic nightmare for Murch. He had his session with Douglas Lumber and said his farewells.

He had a long session with the company attorney about Mike. The lawyer felt that the offer of immediate psychiatric care might influence the court. Through newspaper friends, Murch managed to keep the incident out of print.

The agency staff was informed that Mike was ill. Pete was not so easily put off. He demanded the truth. Murch told him.

"The damned fool!" Pete snapped. "And right when we need him most.'

"His problem's greater than ours," Murch observed.

"Is Lorrie staying on?"

Murch nodded.

"Then we still have a chance," Pete said. "Goddamn it! I was afraid that guy would flip. That finishes him with me."

Murch was noncommittal. He wanted no more disputes. After a few moments Pete calmed down.

"Mickels will wonder," he said. "I'll tell him Mike's ill. We can get by. Mike's expendable."

"You were great pals a few days ago," Murch said drily.

"When it comes to money, I lose pals fast sometimes."

Murch smiled crookedly. "The hard-core businessman, that's you."

Pete had the grace to blush a little. "Don't get me wrong. I feel sorry for him. We have to look after Lorrie, too. Only—the agency has to come first."

"That's what I said," Murch said mockingly. "Don't worry. I don't think he'll be back.'

Rick came in for a fast rundown on the revised script.

A crucial moment came for Murch when he saw him the first time after the night at the beach. He had dreaded this moment, uncertain of his emotions, of his capability for anger, or even violence. The picture of his wife on the bed with the other man was vividly etched in his mind.

When the meeting came, he had the odd feeling that he was an observer, watching two other persons. He knew his wife had become this man's mistress, and he resented the betrayal, but he felt no jealousy or anger. She undoubtedly had made herself available. And Rick Andes had done only what a great many men would do. Murch remembered his own transgression with the wife of a client, and now with Lorrie. Was he any different from Rick Andes?

"If I loved Diana, it would be different," he told himself. "Or if I didn't love Lorrie."

Lorrie had heard from Mike; they'd had a brief, unsatisfactory telephone conversation. He said he intended to stay at the beach indefinitely. She told him he would have to call the attorney, that he was out on bail. He agreed to do so. When she tried to convince him to return and visit a psychiatrtist, he became angry and hung up.

At the office she managed somehow to pick up his work and continue it.

A weekend came and went in an uninterrupted segment of long work hours and no rest. There was some juggling of dates for the presentation at LeLane's, all handled by Pete. He brought in the decision on a Monday.

"It's set," he told Murch. "Thursday afternoon."

The two men dropped their growing antagonism as they faced the deadline of a mutual effort.

"We're about ready," Murch said. "I'll schedule a final run-through for Wednesday—without Rick. That leaves us Thursday morning for last-minute changes."

"Good," Pete said. "What about Rick? Will he be in before then?"

"No need," Murch said. "I'll have Helen call him to be here Thursday morning."

He lunched with Lorrie and they rode to his place afterwards so he could change into fresh clothing. The heat and work and fatigue were making him restless.

The house was hot. He suggested that she wait on the patio until he changed. She shook her head and came close to him.

"You're on edge," she said. "You're driving too hard. You're not going to feel much better simply by changing clothes.'

He smiled and drew her to him. Their kiss was light and then it became deep and intense.

"There's a better way," she said softly.

They made love, using the spare bedroom by mutual agreement.

"Not in your bedroom," she had whispered.

"I know ..."

He had not realized how hungry he was for her until it began, and then it was as fervent and abandoned for her as it was for him.

Afterwards they showered and he put on fresh clothing and they returned to the agency. Their work took on the freshness and speed that comes from relaxed energy.

They had dinner together and then he vetoed returning to the agency for more work. He drove to a neighborhood theater and they sat in semidarkness holding hands like young lovers as they watched a sophisticated comedy.

The next morning Murch felt more refreshed than he had felt for days. He awakened early, breakfasted downtown, and was hard at work when the agency staff began to arrive. Shortly after nine o'clock Bill came to his office.

"Spare a few moments, Murch?"

Murch looked up, smiling. "Certainly."

Bill stood in the open doorway. He stepped back to usher Linda Smith into the office. Murch started to greet her cheerfully when he saw the ugly bruise on her face, and the grim anger in Bill's expression. Bill closed the door and leaned back against it.

"Tell him, Linda," he said.

"Bill—please. It really isn't a federal case. I'm certain it's happened to others. I shouldn't have told you. Besides, he'd had too many drinks. I'm not a child. I—"

"Tell him," Bill said again.

"Let me guess," Murch said quietly. "Our friend Walter Mickels?"

"Who else but?" Bill said tightly.

"I won't be delicate," Murch said. "I'm much too concerned. Linda, did anything else happen?"

"In the old-fashioned phraseology—did he force me? Or, as they put it today, was I the victim of a criminal assault? Is that what you mean?"

"Let's not be flip about it, Linda." Murch's expression reflected his shock and anger. Her defiance and flipness faded from her expression.

"Nothing happened," she said. "I probably wouldn't have told any of this if it had. I don't think I'm a girl who could bring herself to admitting rape—except to her doctor or a judge. But to be slugged because I wouldn't seduce is something else."

"How much do you want to tell me?" Murch asked.

She had taken the chair near his desk, and now she brought out a small purse mirror to inspect her face. She touched the bruise gingerly. "It looks horrible, doesn't it?" she said.

"Tell me," Murch suggested.

"Bill was so right. He warned me about Walt. Only I didn't take the warning very seriously. Besides, I thought I might help the agency. And Pete seemed to think it was all right if I played up to Walt a little. He said to keep it on a business level, of course, but any girl knows that she can help things move along with the use of some personality. Men know it, too. They use their personalities.

"Anyhow, we began to date. He never really made a *serious* pass at me. He talked a good game, but what man doesn't? I simply didn't have any trouble—I mean no more than a girl can handle with a few negatives and hand-removing. I even liked him, Murch. I mean, he *can* be pleasant and interesting."

"So?"

"So last night we visited a few night spots, and then he took me home. He asked if he could come in for a nightcap, and I weakened.

"But after another drink—and we'd had quite a few, I'm afraid—he decided to make like a conquering war lord. It became quite a struggle. Finally he got out of control and—well, he hit me. I screamed and he left—after he had called me a few choice things I'd rather not repeat."

The girl spoke rapidly, trying to maintain a light approach, but her voice trembled. She hesitated and took the cigarette Murch offered her.

"I'm sorry, Murch," she said. "I mean, if I've jeopardized the presentation or alienated him toward the agency. I was just trying to—"

"For God's sake, don't apologize!" Murch erupted. "We should apologize to you. Pete should. He's been pushing this. I'm damned sorry it happened, Linda. And damned angry."

"In all fairness, he was awfully stoned, Murch. I mean, it wasn't exactly a normal situation. Maybe I could be a little bit to blame. I wasn't very diplomatic when he became so insistent,"

"Why should you have been?" Murch snapped.

"One reason we're here," Bill said. "Mickels is in the agency now—with Pete. He stopped by and tried to apologize to Linda."

"And?" Murch asked, glancing at the girl.

She shrugged. "So I was big and understanding. Only I didn't let him linger, and I left him standing in my office when I said I had to see Bill. Of course, Bill overheard enough through the connecting doorway, so when Mickels went out, Bill asked, and I told."

"My doctor is across the street," Murch said. "I wish you'd go over and—"

"It isn't that bad, Murch," Linda protested. "Really ..."

He picked up his telephone and dialed. He talked with the doctor, then put down the telephone and wrote the physician's name on a slip of paper. "He'll see you now," he said. "Maybe he can at least do something about the bruise."

"Murch, I wish you wouldn't make such a fuss."

"On your way," he said. "Mind your boss."

She managed a smile. "Well, any girl has to admit that it *is* nice to be sort of looked after. Thanks, Murch. And please?"

"Please what?"

"No trouble with Walt?"

"I'll try to keep the lid on," he promised.

Bill went out with her and before he could return, Murch went to Pete's office. He heard voices inside and he opened the door. He was confronted by the inquiring eyes of Pete

Lanham and Walter Mickels. He went in and shut the door behind him. He didn't greet either man, but looked squarely at Mickels.

"I just had a talk with Linda," he said.

Mickels smiled nervously. "It isn't as bad as it seems. Just some scuffling. I apologized. Nothing to get excited about, Murch."

"Scuffling, hell!" Murch said. "You tried to rape her."

Mickels stood and pushed his chair back angrily. "That's a damned lie! Did she tell you that?"

"Why else would you slug her, Mickels?"

"She slapped me—it was reflex. I'd been drinking. But I didn't try to get into her goddamned pants by force. That's a lot of—"

"I think you did," Murch said.

"Okay, okay! If that's what you want to think. And why are you so damned steamed up? Because you're sleeping with her and want hands off?"

"Take it easy," Murch said very softly. "You're leading with your chin."

"Don't try to shove me, Murch. I wasn't born yesterday. Neither were you. So the boss does a little shacking with a girl working for him. It wouldn't be the first time that's ever happened. The way that baby teases, she knows what it's for—and how to use it. So don't give me the Sir Galahad bit, Murch. It'd be smarter to share the wealth a little. Nevertheless, if I insulted your private little piece, I'm sorry. I apologize."

Murch hit him. Mickels sprawled back upon the chair and then floundered to the floor.

Pete Lanham scrambled between the two men, pushing Murch back. "You damned fool!" he yelped. "What in hell's wrong with you?"

"Get him out of here," Murch said.

"You bastard," Pete said viciously. "What are you trying to do? Completely screw up our chances of getting that account?"

The smaller man shoved Murch out of the office, and Murch let him, his anger cooling as suddenly as it had come up.

He returned to his office, ignoring the abrupt silence in the agency, and the inquisitive looks. Obviously the skirmish had been heard. Inside his office he slammed the door and jerked open the filing drawer for the bottle of Scotch. He took a long drink, capped the bottle, and returned it to the drawer. He went to a window and stared down into the street.

He supposed he shouldn't have hit the man. It would have been smarter to handle it calmly. After all, the girl actually hadn't been hurt much. She had not been raped. But the insinuation that she was sleeping with him, Murch, finally had snapped the frayed nerves and worn control that Murch had fought to maintain for the past few days.

Calmer now, he wondered if Linda had intimated to Mickels that she might be sleeping with her agency's president? He couldn't believe that. Only—

"Hell!" he said aloud. "Damn it all to hell!" He turned from the window in frustration and went to his desk. He waited for the drink to take effect. After a while he felt better. Maybe he had blown the pitch. On the other hand, it might work in reverse. Walter Mickels might have a difficult time explaining to Old Man Gortzein why Murch Colton had slugged him, and why Linda Smith had a bruise.

The telephone rang. It was Bill Rhodes.

"Nice work, boss," Bill said succinctly and hung up.

Murch managed a grin. There was nothing left to do for the time being but work and wait.

His wait was short. Pete came into the office a half-hour later.

"You really ripped it this time," Pete said angrily.

"Let's not go over it again," Murch said wearily. "It either kills us or he keeps his mouth shut. I think he'll keep his mouth shut. He wouldn't want Gortzein to know. It might even help us."

"What in hell was Linda trying to do?" Pete demanded.

"Probably trying to keep from getting raped," Murch said evenly. "Offhand, I'd say that would be her prerogative."

"Knock it off, Murch. So maybe the guy had been drinking, and they'd had a night of it, and they're in her apartment and there's a bed there, so he wants to get into her pants. So that's a reason for her to slug him?"

"Aren't you getting it backwards, Pete? She's carrying the bruise."

"So he slaps her back. A teaser has that coming. The point is—"

"The point is, you're getting under my skin, Pete. I mean it. I don't know where we stand with the pitch, but I'm going ahead. I don't think Mickels could stop us—or would have the guts to try, under the circumstances. But when it's over, win or lose, you and I and Harold, when he gets back, are going to have a long talk."

"Don't be too sure," Pete said tightly. "If we don't get LeLane's—particularly with Douglas Lumber gone—you won't have much to talk about. And if we get LeLane's, I'll be the account executive. Let's not kid about that. So you'll have even less to talk about."

He turned abruptly and walked out of the office.

Wearily Murch got up and closed the door.

Pete Lanham returned to his own office. He lit a cigarette and thoughtfully stared at his desk top. Finally he settled his glasses firmly on his nose and reached for a telephone. He dialed.

"Mr. Gortzein," he said, "this is Pete Lanham. I'd like to see you for a few moments—at once. I have shocking information that I think you should know about. He carefully selected his words, trying to obtain an appointment without revealing his reason.

"You can't tell me over the phone, yet?" Gortzein asked.

"I think it's too important to you—I'll only take moments."

"Then all right. In twenty minutes, maybe? I'll tell the girl she should bring you right in."

Gortzein had spared no expense in the décor for his office. The desk was large, the drapes were rich, the colors obviously selected by a decorator. Pete had never seen the office before. He was impressed.

"You like it?" Gortzein asked, noting Pete's quick inspection.

"Yes," Pete said in oversimplification.

"It cost too much," the old man said. "But you control the company, who's to object?" He waved his visitor to a chair.

"So?" he said. "You have some information?"

"Not very happy, I'm afraid," said Pete. "Actually, I hesitated to call you, but decided it's the only ethical thing to do—even if it may jeopardize our presentation."

"So now you built up the scene," Gortzein said, "maybe now the information?"

Pete took a long, slow, deep breath, partly to steady himself, partly for effect. He wanted to create the image of substantiality, and an executive-to-executive manner.

"We've had an unpleasantness involving one of your men and a girl at the agency," he began. "It appears that it was a case of attempted rape and—"

"Talk plain, Pete," Gortzein said. "You mean Mickels has been at it again? Who'd he try to lay this time? That Smith girl?"

Pete's eyes narrowed in quick thought. His thunder wasn't as great as he thought it would be.

"It's a little worse this time, perhaps," he said. "Linda has a bruised face. This one could be a police matter. Murch was so angry he knocked Mickels down. I got things under control. But you have dynamite in Walt Mickels, Mr. Gortzein. Sooner or later he could well do something that would reflect upon LeLane's."

Gortzein watched the younger man with eyes that held a slightly amused expression, and the blasé calmness that comes from a great many years of living, observing and understanding.

"So Murch Colton hit him?" Gortzein said. "Hard?"

"Yes," Pete admitted.

Gortzein sighed. "That's good. Linda's a nice girl. I like her. I've watched her copy on The Smart Shop. You people don't know how good she is, maybe."

"Indeed we do, Mr. Gortzein. That's why I've had her out here quite a bit—to get the feel of your line. And I guess that's why Mickels got the wrong idea."

Gortzein sighed. "Mickels went too far this time. Before, so he makes passes. So what man hasn't? But beating up sweet young things like Linda Smith. Tell me, she hurt bad?"

"No, but the bruise looks bad. It's none of my business, Mr. Gortzein, but I do think that Mickels is in a position to harm your firm irrevocably."

Gortzein held up a gnarled hand in a silencing gesture. "So Mickels is fired. When he lays a hand on a girl like Linda, he's out. That satisfy you?"

"I don't like to be the one who—"

"You're lying," Gortzein said bluntly. "This doesn't hurt your agency. Maybe it helps because maybe you think now I owe you something? Maybe you think I'll feel guilty?"

"Not at all. Murch deliberately placed the agency in jeopardy when he knocked Mickels down. But it only substantiates our stand that we are ethical, honest people, living and working in your own community. We are loyal to our employees and—"

"Young man, you should learn yet not to make speeches. Now, you got something else on your mind? This build-up is not from when knighthood was in flower. What do you really want?"

Pete had not expected the old man to so readily put a finger on the hidden spring, but he had. There was one way to play it, if he wanted to take the gamble. He decided he would.

"I want Mickels' job. I can do it better for you than he did. I'll want more money, plus a bonus, a stock deal, and the rest of the fringe benefits."

"You ask a lot in a hurry," Gortzein commented.

"I know what I want, and I'm not out of a job. I own part of an agency. I don't need you as much as you need me."

"So what else? The job and then maybe give the account to Murch Colton?"

"Not necessarily. You and I would have to add up the score and make a decision."

"How do I know you wouldn't work behind my back? You know what you're doing to Murch Colton."

Pete pushed his glasses into place and leaned forward, looking at the older man very earnestly.

"Mr. Gortzein, I'm ambitious. I am not selling out Murch Colton. I might still decide he would have the best agency for us, even if I were not with them any longer. I would work for *your* best interests—my loyalties would be to my employer. You must remember that I'm not bargaining against Murch— and he's not my employer. I own part of the firm—which I would have to sell, of course. I am simply changing the direction of my career. I would rather work for LeLane's—for you—than to be part owner of the agency."

"How much do you want?"

"Twenty thousand to start, plus a bonus—such as you already give, and you might as well know I've been checking because I'm interested—plus a stock deal."

"I've been overpaying Mickels twelve. I'll start you at sixteen, with the bonus, the stock deal, and benefits. You deliver and you get a thousand a year raise until you ceiling at twenty. Then we talk again.

"What strings?"

"Only one," Gortzein said. "This continues so long as LeLane's sales increase five per cent every year—except any year if the designers blow the styles or we got trouble you can't help."

"I'll take it," Pete said.

The two men smiled and shook hands.

"So now I'm working for you?"

"Unload your agency stock, we make the deal."

Pete shook his head. "That isn't necessary. I'm working for you now."

"All right. What you want to know? What agency I like?"

Pete nodded.

"Kate Rhodes and CWC. She's smart, she thinks big, and she's got one of the biggest agencies behind her. Next—you people. Two reasons. That Lorrie McPherson, she's good. She's worked for us. I like her work. Second, your almost-raped Linda Smith. She writes fashion copy like no one else I've seen in a long time. So it's almost even. I'll admit you were a factor at your agency. I didn't just hire you because you cut Walt Mickels' throat. You're ambitious and greedy and ruthless. This I can use, if it's working for me. As long as you don't turn out to be a *schnook* like Mickels."

"But it's not definitely decided about the agencies?"

"No. I got to see the presentations."

"It's understood that I do not report this to Murch."

"If it is not understood, would I be telling you?"

Pete nodded. "Good. I'll resign immediately from the agency. I assume you want me to take over the advertising department at once?"

Gortzein nodded. "One thing. I don't have to like you to hire you and pay you to make money for me. Maybe I will like you. Who knows? Only I'll never be sure that maybe you didn't tell that *goniff* Mickels that Linda would go to bed with him. But if you're smart enough to set this up, maybe you're smart enough to sell LeLane's like it should be sold. So." He shrugged and dismissed Lanham with a nod.

Pete went out to his car. He got in and took a long, deep drag of smoke.

So the old man liked Kate and CWC—and he liked Linda's copy, and Lorrie's work. Well, probably nothing could be done about Lorrie. She was stuck. But Linda was ambitious. Working for CWC would be the first rung to heaven for her. She'd leave Murch in a second for a chance like that. And with Kate working as account executive, and with necessary trips to the CWC office in New York for Pete Lanham, and important contacts, and the chance to establish himself—maybe a man like Pete Lanham could end up in the big time as an account executive with CWC. It often happened that way, and already he'd made the first important step.

I think I'll call Kate Rhodes, he told himself. *I might make a little deal to start things—suggest she hire Linda to give me leverage with Old Man Gortzein in throwing the account to CWC; and with a combination like that, how can I lose?"*

CHAPTER TEN

WEDNESDAY MORNING a local radio announcer said: "The hot spell continues unbroken. Up to 101 degrees is expected this afternoon. No immediate relief is in sight …"

Forest fires burned south of Douglas City. The morning newspaper reported four cases of heat prostration and an impending water shortage.

At the beach, Diana Colton awoke shortly before eight o'clock, still conscious of Rick Andes' weight beside her in the bed, although he had left silently before daybreak. She stared at the bedroom ceiling and made a decision. The telephone call the night before had paved the way for her. She wanted Rick Andes permanently, and now she knew how to get her freedom first, and possibly Rick Andes a little later. She decided to go to the city.

Lorrie McPherson, in her home on the heights, took a shower and then went into a bedroom. She stood nude before a mirror and looked at herself a little self-consciously, thinking how many times she had read books in which an author used that situation as an excuse to describe the intimate details of a woman's body.

Well, she could look at her own body in the privacy of her bedroom with the knowledge that this was the body Murch had seen and loved, and she was proud of it! She dressed quickly. Mike had not returned, nor had he phoned. There had been a brief note, however, in which he bluntly had suggested divorce.

He would be in the city in a week or so. The thing with the police was under control.

In her small apartment Linda Smith decided against even the lightest girdle. It would be too hot today. She selected cool linen separates because they were smart and she was going to have lunch with Kate Rhodes. She wondered why Kate had called her the previous night. She had sounded mysterious, and what had she meant by, "Something of real interest to you?"

After she dressed she again inspected the bruise on her face. She had experimented with make-up and dark glasses so that it wasn't quite so obvious.

Murch had been terribly angry. It was the first time a man had ever fought because of her. The physical violence had sickened her a little when she heard about it, but there had been a strange thrill to know that Murch had punished Walt Mickels.

Walt had intended to rape her. She was certain of that, and she remembered it with mixed emotions. She had teased him. She had let him think she might go to bed with him. But she was only teasing. She didn't want to go to bed with Walt Mickels. So maybe she deserved to be hit, and she almost grudgingly admired him for it. And Murch had knocked him down.

She smiled secretly to herself as she thought, *Murch couldn't really rape me. I think I'd be too willing!*

It was one of the secret thoughts that always made her slightly ashamed of herself. She put it firmly out of her mind and left the small apartment, thinking: *I wonder why Kate wants to see me? I wonder if I'll ever be as successful as she is. Think of working for CWC!*

As Linda left her apartment, Murch finished his café breakfast. He walked toward the agency. It was hot again. He unbuttoned the jacket of his summer-weight suit to let air circulate.

Pete Lanham was in his office. He came out as soon as he heard Murch and Murch wondered why the small man was there so early.

"Anything wrong?" he asked.

"Wrong?" Pete asked, slightly puzzled.

"You're here so early."

"Good reason," Pete said. "I want to talk with you, Murch."

"Again? That tone, Pete—what are you sore about now?"

"Not a thing in the world," Pete said. "I'm leaving the agency."

"What's this all about?" Murch asked quietly.

"Beginning today I'm the new director of advertising at LeLane's," Pete said. "Mickels is out. That bit with Linda finished him. Their offer is too good to pass up, Murch. I'm sorry, but that's how it is."

"You can't just walk out like this! You owe something to the agency and your accounts."

Pete shrugged. "Tough," he agreed. "But a man has to look out for himself. I'm under no contract. You can service the accounts until you get someone."

Murch was thinking rapidly, estimating what the corporation—the agency—would have to pay Lanham for his stock. It would be a substantial amount, just when the agency needed every cent to even stay in business. This could well hurt the firm."

"All right," he said calmly, "that's that. Now the big question."

"Your presentation?" Pete asked.

"It was yours up until now," Murch commented grimly. "Okay, *my* presentation. What can we expect?"

"The same consideration I'll give the others, Murch. I'm sorry I can't promise more, but now my loyalty necessarily must be to LeLane's."

"Knock it off, Pete. You can give me a straighter answer than that."

"I can't, Murch. That's the truth. I can tell you—in confidence—that CWC is strong. Also that Gortzein likes Linda Smith's copy and Lorrie's work. From there, I can't tell you anything more."

Murch eyed him narrowly, knowing that Pete probably reflected Gortzein's thinking.

"You're moving over there today?" he asked.

"This morning. I'm sorry as hell it has to be this way—"

"You're not sorry," Murch said without humor, "but good luck, Pete. Maybe you'll need it."

"I doubt it," Pete said. "Do you want to break the news to the staff, or shall I?"

"I'll make the announcement," Murch said shortly.

He did, a half-hour later. He met with Bill, Lorrie, Linda and Helen. They took the news in silence. This time Murch had not included the stenographers and lower echelon of the staff. Helen could pass on the news to them as she saw fit.

"We'll be in a bind on production," he told Helen. "Can you handle it for a few days?"

"I can try."

"Good. Well find someone to help until Harold returns. Bill, will you help me on a few of Pete's accounts temporarily?"

"Sure," Bill said. He looked worried. Murch knew the copy chief recognized all the implications in Pete's resignation.

Lorrie said, "If there's anything I can do ..."

Murch said, "We have to decide if we're going on with the presentation." He told them about his conversation with Pete. "So there it is," he concluded. "CWC is strong. We have strength in you, Lorrie, and in Linda."

Bill said, "I say we pitch with what we have."

Suddenly Murch realized that he was sick of the presentation. Maybe it was because he had worked too long and hard on it, or because Pete and Mike had dreamed it up and were now out of the picture, or because his knowledge about his wife and Rick Andes might be coloring his thoughts.

"I don't know," he said. "It doesn't entirely reflect us as an agency now. Pete will be gone. Probably Mike, too." He looked at Lorrie. She nodded.

No one spoke. They watched him silently and after a moment he said emphatically, "You're right, Bill. We go with what we have."

The meeting broke up, and Bill detained Murch for a moment.

Bill said, "I know what this can do to us financially. Is the agency obligated to buy back his stock?"

"Yes. It's a common arrangement in agencies."

"Most places I've been," Bill said. "So I'll put my neck out. We have a good shop. I have a few thousand. I'll pick up some of that stock—if you and Harold would like me in."

Murch looked at the thin, tired-appearing man and felt a deep friendship for him.

"It's a gamble," he said.

"I didn't ask that," Bill countered. "Interested?"

"Definitely yes! We'll talk about it after the pitch."

Murch felt better as he returned to his office. Maybe they had a fighting chance.

Shortly after eleven o'clock Diana came into his office.

He was surprised. "I didn't expect to see you today!"

"Probably not," she said, fussing around in a handbag for cigarettes. "I'm full of surprises today."

This was the first time he had confronted his wife since he had so graphically witnessed her infidelity. He wondered what she would say if she knew.

Abruptly he realized he didn't particularly care. It seemed that everything had been erased between them. He saw her through different eyes. And the memories were inconsequential. Nothing between them was of importance. She was almost like a stranger to him and oddly without appeal.

She continued to smile. "I understand you're quite the gallant knight. I had an interesting telephone call last night. So now you've taken to knocking men down because they make passes at your mistress!"

Anger pierced him. "That's a damned lie! Who? Mickels?"

"Does it matter who told me? Let's ask Linda if it's true."

"Leave Linda out of this," he snapped.

"Why should I? If I'm going to ask for a divorce—and I am— she should know all the ugly little stories making the rounds: that she broke up a marriage; that you brawl in public over her. Before I'm through, everyone will know what she is, a tart—and what you are. And I think I'd like a single settlement. I'll take the house, my car, and a sizable portion of our bank account, the stock we bought, and a few other things."

He stared at her, hardly believing what he was hearing. Now that she was the mistress of an ex-football pro, she wanted out from her marriage, and she wanted everything she could get. In a single moment of recollection he realized that she had always wanted everything she could get. Abruptly he laughed.

Harsh anger lines came to her mouth and around her eyes. "You can't deny that you knocked a man down over that little bitch," she said. "There are too many witnesses."

"You can have your divorce," he assured her. "Gladly. But no settlement, and you'll leave Linda alone. She hasn't anything to do with this. There is someone but never mind who it is."

She looked at him narrowly, and a small cat-smile twisted her lips. "Lorrie McPherson!" she said. "I might have known.

I saw Mike at the beach. He said you and Lorrie were working together—that she thinks a lot of you. He was acting oddly, and he's running around with that Laddie creature, but I didn't add it up until now. You and Lorrie!"

Suddenly he was disgusted with the whole thing. He wanted to walk out of the agency, take Lorrie with him, get in a car and drive.

Diana smiled mockingly. "One corespondent is as good as another. A good private detective should find something, somewhere."

Murch frowned, thinking that a private detective might trace Lorrie and him to the night at the motel.

He said, "You'll have your divorce, Diana, but on *my* terms. You're going to do nothing to Lorrie and me. That's too clean for you to soil."

"Won't I?" she taunted. "And why not?"

"Because the night Mike went down to the beach, Lorrie and I went after him. We got there very early in the morning. We thought we'd get you up to help find him. We went in with my key. We didn't awaken you, Diana. We didn't think it would be sporting to awaken you and Rick from such a sound sleep in the nude. So if you want to bring up indiscretions, I *do* have a witness!"

Diana's face paled. Her tongue licked nervously at her lips.

"All right," she finally said, "so you know, and now we're even. The difference is that I'm getting a man and she's getting nothing. You never were the man Rick Andes is. You never had the pure masculine drive and strength and ability to make a woman want to scream with the joy of it. You! God, she's welcome to you!

"But I'm going to sue you and ask for all I can get. You won't stop me because you won't want me to drag your dear Lorrie through the mud—make her testify that she saw your wife on a bed just after I'd been laying another man! Not you, Murch. Not the dragon slayer!"

"Name her in a suit and I'll never rest until I'd destroyed both you and Rick Andes."

"Let's put it this way," she said. "I'll sue for incompatibility, in Reno—and you *will* make a nice settlement. Then I won't name your baby-doll. *I won't make things all muddy if you play along.* I'm a changed woman now, Murch darling. I'm what's known as a sweet-laying bitch. Suddenly I like it that way."

And looking at her he realized she spoke the truth.

"All right," he said in a low, angry voice. "Now get out. We've had it."

She got up and carefully put out her cigarette. "It will be a pleasure," she said sweetly. "A distinct pleasure."

He waited until he was certain that she had left the agency and then went to the art room. Lorrie regarded him with worried eyes.

"Diana?" she said. "She looked furious."

He told her what had happened. Lorrie listened quietly. "Oh, Murch," she murmured. "It's all so ... sordid."

"Please don't worry about it. I had to protect Linda, and she guessed about you and me. Mike probably said something, and she had to know sooner or later. Your note from Mike—suggesting a divorce—now this. Don't you see, Lorrie? We're almost in the clear."

She nodded and gazed into his face. "You love me, Murch? You truly love me?"

"Yes, I truly love you. I want you. I need you."

"All right, Murch."

She glanced at the closed door and then went to him. They kissed quickly in a mutual gesture of relief, hunger and love.

"Suddenly I'm glad," she whispered. "Terribly glad!"

❧ ❧ ❧

Linda returned late from lunch and walked into the agency wearing an odd, triumphant smile. She went directly to Bill's office. He looked up from his typewriter and grinned.

"So?" he asked.

"Bill, is Murch in? I mean, is he in so that you and I can talk with him? It's terribly important."

"Not Mickels again?" Bill said, his smile gone.

"No, not that. Only … can we talk with Murch?"

"Sure. He's in. Want to tell me first?"

She shook her head.

They went to Murch's office and he greeted them cheerfully. "Linda, your bruise is going fast," he observed.

"It really wasn't too bad, Murch," she said. She glanced nervously at Bill. I think I'd better tell you something, both of you."

Murch's smile also faded. "Mickels hasn't—?"

"No. I wish you weren't so sweet—I mean, it makes it so terribly difficult."

"Makes what difficult?" Murch asked reassuringly.

Linda took a deep breath and said rapidly, "I had lunch with Kate Rhodes. CWC has offered me a job in New York. It's everything I want. I mean, I just couldn't say no. I'll go to New York at once. She's already talked with them. They want me no matter who gets the LeLane's account. They have some soap and food accounts where Kate thinks I'll be good. She's read my Smart Shop copy and—well, I guess that's all. I mean, I'll have to resign at once because she wants me to leave next week."

Murch wondered how much of this could be attributed to Mickels, or to Pete Lanham. Someone probably had told Kate that Gortzein liked Linda. This would strengthen the CWC pitch; and even if they missed, they still were getting a good copywriter.

At least, he was glad that Linda was getting the break—if that was what she wanted.

Linda watched them anxiously, blushing and embarrassed.

"I think it's a wonderful break for you," Murch said.

"Then you aren't angry? I mean, because of the presentation?"

Despite her concern about the ethics of the situation, Murch detected steel in the girl's voice. What they thought didn't matter too much to her now that a New York career was within her grasp.

"We hate to lose you," he said. "But the only way to go ahead in this business is to go ahead."

She looked at Bill. He grinned crookedly and said, "That's a rough league up there. But you'll make it."

She relaxed and smiled happily. "You're wonderful! Both of you! Simply wonderful!"

A few moments later Murch and Bill were alone. Bill shook his head. "That Kate," he said. "She doesn't miss many tricks."

"Linda's good," Murch said. "You can't blame Kate—or CWC. Good talent is hard to come by."

"And where does that leave us?" Bill asked.

Murch replied, "As the old saying goes—just a little farther up the creek without a paddle."

By noon the mercury registered 101 degrees and was still climbing. At a little after one o'clock, Diana Colton drove over the crest of the coastal mountains and began the descent to the beach. The sea air was only slightly cooler. The sky was cloudless. The beaches were well populated.

She drove to her apartment, had a quick lunch, and changed into the bikini.

On the way to the beach she glanced toward the apartments when Rick was staying. She did not see him, but she saw a sports car with a California license. It could be coincidence, but a girl from California had visited Rick before.

Diana looked anxiously at Rick's windows. The drapes were not drawn. The place looked deserted. She turned toward the beach.

They were on a large blanket and Rick was spreading sun lotion on the girl's bare back. The girl was stretched out face down, her back trim and smooth, her buttocks tight and rounded, her long and slim legs spread slightly in the manner of sun bathers.

Jealous anger had been alien to Diana's nature until this moment, but now she felt its furious, stinging lash. She instinctively wanted to approach them, to challenge the girl's right to be with Rick Andes, to challenge his right to put his hand on the smooth, brown back, or to look at the compact, rounded buttocks, or to lazily enjoy the presence of a young female.

She fought down the impulse and returned to her apartment. She found binoculars and sat in the window to watch the couple. They remained on the beach only a short time and then returned to Rick's apartment. Diana went out and took a position from which she could view his windows. She saw him draw the drapes.

In seething anger she walked the beach and waited ... An hour later the girl came out. She was dressed in shorts and halter and she carried a beach bag. Rick kept an arm about her as they walked to the sports car. The girl got in, turned her face up to be kissed and drove away. Rick went back to his apartment.

Diana left the beach and followed him. He came to the door looking sleepy.

"Hi," he said "You're back early."

"I've been back since one," she answered tightly. "I didn't want to interrupt. Who is she?"

She entered the apartment as she talked, her gaze darting about. Through an open doorway she saw his bed. It looked mussed. He watched her scrutiny with amusement.

"A friend."

Diana walked past him and into the bedroom. She looked at the mussed bed and the pillow on the floor.

"Is she good?" she asked Rick.

"Cool off, baby," he said. "This doesn't buy you anything."

"You deny it?"

"If you want me to."

"Let's find out, Rick. Let's see just how enthusiastic you can be." Angrily she got out of the halter and the bikini and stood defiantly nude by the bed. "Even *you* aren't indefatigable! I know you, Rick—how it is the first time, and the second, and sometimes the third. Now let's see how good she was."

He laughed. She fell back onto the bed. "Prove it, Rick."

"Christ! You act like a kook! I don't want to lay you. I don't feel like it."

"Would you feel like laying *her* again?"

"What are you trying to prove? Get up and dress."

"Maybe you'd like to try again later?"

"I've a date later."

"With her?"

His eyes narrowed. "Don't push, baby. It's been fun. You're good in the hay, but I don't want to play for keeps. I never will. And you're getting a little tiresome with this act."

She got up angrily and put on the halter and bikini. He watched her with an amused expression so that she became furious in her anger. She sprang at him, her fingers scratching.

"Damn you!" she cried. "Damn you!"

He held her motionless. "Shut up! I don't like a brawling, yelling, scratching, jealous bitch. So shut up."

His words sobered her. She stood back, breathing heavily.

"Listen to me, Rick," she said. "I had it out with Murch today. We're getting a divorce."

"So?"

"So he and Lorrie McPherson came down here early one morning. They walked in on us when we were together in my bed. So you're not in such a good spot, Rick. You could have a hell of a scandal."

He regarded her thoughtfully. "There won't be a scandal," he said. "He wouldn't want that. He wouldn't want to drag Lorrie into it. He goes for her. I've seen it during our sessions. And Lorrie and Mike are finished."

"Rick, I've given you more than I've given any man. You're not cheating on me with some little tramp from California."

He smiled crookedly. "You've got it all wrong, Diana. You were very much available and I'm a man—I took what you were so anxious to give away. Does that make you a tramp, too? As a matter of fact, I'm going back to California with her tonight. A change of scenery would be nice."

"You've got a job to do tomorrow," she reminded him.

"Oh, that. Well … I'm embarrassed now, knowing he walked in on us. And I never did like the idea. But I'll be ethical." He glanced at his watch, picked up a telephone and placed a call. She glared at him silently.

"Is Murch there?" he said into the phone. "Oh? When will he be back? … Never mind. Helen, tell Murch that Rick Andes called. I've suddenly been called to California. I'll have to cancel out on the pitch tomorrow. No, there's no use him calling back. He hasn't paid me anything. He doesn't owe me anything. Just tell him I'm sorry."

He hung up.

Bill missed Murch's call about Rick Andes because he was having dinner with Kate. It had started with a call from her and an invitation for a quick drink after work. They had met in the hotel cocktail lounge.

"We present in the morning," she said. "I may leave immediately after word is handed out. So I thought we might have one for the road."

"That isn't exactly why I accepted," he said. "And I'll pick up the tab. I have a question or two."

"Linda?"

"Certainly."

"I heard that Mr. Gortzein likes her work," Kate told him. "Actually, we were already interested in her. So I talked with New York. We decided to hire her." Kate sipped her drink. "One thing—I know she's well trained. You're a good copy chief and a good teacher."

He shrugged. "I only hope you're hiring her because of her talent, and not because you think you need a squeeze play to help grab the account."

"You'd hate to see her cast upon the waters of Madison Avenue without a job if we miss? No, Bill, I wouldn't do that to a gal."

"Wouldn't you?" he asked.

She was amused by his skepticism. "Honestly, I wouldn't. And anyhow, I can say it in this case because she *is* good—and ambitious. We can use her on several accounts."

Bill sighed. "I guess I was just testing." They had finished their drinks, and he indicated the empty glasses. "More?"

"No. But I'm hungry."

"I'll buy your dinner."

They ate, keeping conversation within the safe areas of small talk. Afterwards, they walked out into the summer evening.

"Ride?" he suggested.

"I'd love it."

He drove the skyline highway and parked where the valley spread below them. Dusk was near and a few lights were on. Kate rested her head back and looked at the horizon.

"Bill, what are you going to pitch tomorrow?" she asked. "You can tell me now—I couldn't do anything about it. I'm just curious, now that you've lost Pete Lanham and Linda. You don't have much left."

"We have a pitch."

"But *what?*"

"I was hoping you wouldn't ask."

"I'm only making conversation, Bill."

Suddenly he was sick of the whole business. How many years had it been? The constant competition, throat-cutting, back-stabbing, pressuring. How long does a man take it calmly? How long does he pretend sophistication before he erupts in anger?

"You're not making conversation, Kate. You really want to know. With that female, steel-trap mind of yours, you could raise hell with us even before we got in there. It won't work, Kate. No dice."

"I don't think I like the inference, Bill," she said curtly.

He turned and faced her. Quietly he said, "Before we married, while we were, and after we were divorced, you used that phrase with me. You hadn't liked the 'inference' of this or that or something else that I'd mentioned. And it suddenly occurs to me that I've been running from these words, dreading the possibility of displeasing you, offending you, crossing you. Do you know why? I'll tell you. Because I've loved you. Before, since and after. I've loved you, and you've known it. And when it pleased you, you used it. But it's time for a change."

She sat up. "I don't like the—as you put it—'inference' of this whole conversation any longer. You'd better take me back."

"No. You're going to listen. We're going to look at us."

"We're going back to the hotel."

"We're going to look at me: a fair copy chief, starting to age around the corners, but still doing a good job. No great prize, no great success, but a reasonably happy guy, except that I love my ex-wife.

"And let's look at you, Kate: a hell of a success; in *Ad Age* every couple of weeks; earning a top salary; a power in the business. But let's look a little closer. You're also crowding forty now. You probably don't want to remarry—or you would have.

"I don't know what you've done about your sex life. Something, I suppose. You're hot-blooded, so it's a factor. And what do you do when you leave that plush New York office each evening? Go home to an apartment? Sit and watch television? Take in some shows? Go to concerts? Don't try to convince me that you lead a gay, wild life of carefree joy. You can't and handle the job you're on—"

"Bill, you have no right to—"

"Oh, shut up," he said wearily. "That's another of your damned clichés. 'You have no right to—' Goddamn it, I do have a right! You've done enough to my life. Actually, I should shake the hell out of you; even slap you around—if I were a couple of status symbols lower. I've loved you like hell ever since I met you; I've taken everything you dished out; I sacrificed my marriage so that you could have a career; I let you take the lead—but I'm sick of the back seat."

"I don't think that you—"

"Look, Kate—I've turned down New York spots. Did you know that? Turned them down because I don't like what those jobs do to people. You're not impressing me with your position. You never have. I like it here—with a small agency. And now you think you can soft-talk me out of our angles on the pitch. You've stolen Linda. And you're probably playing ball with Mickels. I suppose he has an eye on a berth with CWC. Only it's not—"

Now she faced him, eyes blazing. "If you were offered something in New York you'd have taken it. Otherwise why this great scene? Are you jealous of my career? Is that it? Do you begrudge my success while you've been anchored to a small-time agency?"

He began an angry retort, but suddenly shook his head. "Skip it," he said. "You wouldn't understand. The simple, damned, stupid fact that I love you."

"It is not stupid" she snapped. Then she looked startled and was silent, her eyes searching his face.

"Oh, yes, it is," he said quietly. "Because I'm going to grow old loving you, taking my one-night stands with one woman or another until that loses its attraction, and then filling my time with some damned hobby. But there's something you've missed. I'm going to buy in with Murch; help him build as sweet a small agency as you'll find west of Madison Avenue. And I've decided about you."

"What?"

"You can go to hell, Kate."

He reached for the ignition key, but her hand stopped him.

"Wait," she said. "I said it wasn't stupid for you to love me. Why? Why did I say that, Bill?"

"I long ago gave up trying to fathom your motivations."

"I think I know. I think I've never wanted you to stop. That I really asked to come out here to pitch the LeLane's account because I wanted to see you again. Not to compete with you, but to see you. Suddenly our short visit in New York wasn't enough."

He gazed at her, his face strangely without expression. "Go on," he said. "What else?"

"The next step is yours, Bill."

He took her shoulders in his hands and turned her so that she faced him. Slowly and deliberately he kissed her with a violence that left her gasping for breath.

"Bill, more—so we'll know," she sobbed, pressing herself against him in unexpected abandon.

Dusk was upon them and cars drove by. He kissed her again and felt the feverish response. He looked about him, opened a door and got out. He went around the car and opened the door for her. She stood beside him, searching his face with eyes that were ashine with tears.

He took her hand and they walked into the forest until it became dark in the heavy undergrowth.

They found a place sheltered by ferns and carpeted with grass. He laid her down gently and kissed her until she lay back, eyes shut, lips parted. He found the buttons of her dress, discovered with pleasure the garter belt instead of the girdle, the firmness of flesh, smoothness of skin, and finally the wildly sweet triumph of entrance and possession.

"Oh, Bill ... so long," she gasped. "So terribly long a time ... and so badly needed ... and please ... oh, please ... please ... please ... I love you ... oh, now ... !

Much later they returned to the car. They smoked in contentment before he started the engine.

"You don't doubt it?" she asked.

"No, Kate. And it's time to ask, now that the other is burned out for the moment: Are you coming back to me?"

"Of course. I've hated it back there, Bill. But I've been proud. And I've loved a career. Only it's time now. And there are new careers to be had out here."

"Like a good small agency?"

"I have a few thousand to invest, if you want another principal."

"I'll buy that. I think Murch will, too. And about tomorrow?"

"No quarter, Bill. Isn't that the correct way? I'll pitch my heart out for them."

"I wouldn't want it any other way."

"Don't tell Murch until it's over. This is just ours."

He nodded. "It's damned high time a few things became *ours* again …"

Murch received his message from Rick Andes when he returned to the office very late that afternoon. Helen looked extremely worried. She had waited for him.

"I tried to find you," she said. "I called everywhere."

"I was getting a haircut," he told her. "He said there's no use calling back?"

"Yes. Murch—what are we going to do?"

He sank down in a chair, looked around the empty office and back at Helen Vaughan. "Has Bill left?"

She nodded. "Before Rick Andes called."

"See if you can catch him at his apartment."

She dialed and waited. There was no answer. She hung up and looked questioningly at him.

"Lorrie?"

"She left a few moments after Bill did."

Murch sighed wearily. "Okay, Helen. You may as well leave. There's nothing we can do about it right now."

"Murch—I realize how terrible this is—just before the presentation. I'll be home if you need me. And I can get one or two of the girls. Just call."

"Thanks, Helen. I don't know what we'll do yet. I'll have to think it through."

He went back to his office and sat at his desk. He felt beaten, battered, drained. Vaguely he wondered if he and Bill could give the pitch. It was tailored to a different type of person. It would go sour.

Helen had given him a night connection, and he dialed Lorrie's number. She answered at once. He quickly told her what had happened.

"Come out here to eat with me," she said. "I'm only having ham and eggs, but they should do. We can talk."

"That's a good, constructive idea," he said, forcing lightness into his voice. "I'll bring the client's bottle."

They had two drinks before she put on the ham and eggs. He went into the kitchen with her, mixing a third drink for them, and watched her prepare their meal.

She worked quickly, competently, with no fuss. She wore shorts in the lingering heat of the day, and he enjoyed looking at her long legs and gracefully rounded thighs.

"You're a lovely woman," he said.

"Let's discuss the pitch," she urged, and began to set the table.

"What pitch? We don't have one now. Remember? It was built around Rick Andes—and now we have no Rick."

"We have a pitch," she said. "It's there somewhere. We can't have done all this work without having something to present."

"It's all tailored for Rick Andes. There's no other outside talent available."

They explored the problem in greater detail as they ate, and afterwards on the patio.

Finally she said, "Murch, shouldn't we be at the office doing something about it?"

He stared at her thoughtfully and then he shook his head. "Lorrie, it's no use. I'm beat—on edge—angry—everything I shouldn't be to do a three- or four-day job in a few hours."

She considered his words, stretching her long legs out and scrutinizing the tips of her sandaled toes. Suddenly she stood and extended a hand to him. "Come," she said.

Slightly puzzled, he followed her. She took him into the house and opened a door. "This is the guest room in *this* house," she said. "This isn't my bed, but it's a very comfortable one."

He remembered that she had insisted upon the guest room in his home. He looked down at her and smiled. He kissed her lightly on the forehead and then traced his lips along the silver streak in her hair. "You're a very understanding woman," he said.

She laughed softly. "Since I've been old enough to know how men talk, and the so-called facts of life, it seems to me that men always are saying, 'What that girl needs is a damned good lay!' Of course, that's simply a man's way of rationalizing his own needs! I'm not sure any woman ever really needed that in the way men mean it. But I think there are times when it's exactly what a man may need from his girl. And I'm your girl, Murch."

"My wonderful girl, you mean!" he said softly.

"You get ready. I'll be back in a few moments."

She left him and when she returned shortly afterwards she wore a dark silken robe. "The doors are all bolted," she said. "Mike's at the beach. He called me just before you came—asked me to send some clothing down to him, and said again that he wants a divorce. So we're all safe and sound, theoretically free, and barricaded from the world for a while. Later we can talk about the presentation."

He looked at her from the bed. A faint breeze came in through the high window of the room, cooling it slightly.

"Right now," he said, "we have other things to do."

"That's why I'm here," she assured him. She took off the robe, letting it fall deliberately from her shoulders to her feet, and she stood quietly while he looked at her. She posed for half a moment and then walked toward him.

He pulled her to him as soon as she came to him on the smooth, cool sheet, and for an instant she welcomed his arms and mouth. Then she gently drew away from him.

"Relax," she whispered. "Shut your eyes. Let me …"

"It's a lot to ask," he smiled. "I want you so much—"

"I know," she said. "But this is *my* time, darling."

She firmly pushed him back so that he rested flat, his head upon a pillow. He looked up into her face and saw an infinite female wisdom in her eyes, and a promise of unstinted abandon.

"Shut your eyes," she said again.

He obeyed her and seconds later he felt the first soft explorations of her mouth and hands. He had known the intimacies of awakening a woman to complete readiness, but never before had he known the subtleness with which a woman could build passion in a man.

After a time the last of inhibitions became memories, and now they sought a complete devotion to service, one to the other, as they deliberately denied themselves consummation until the demands transcended all restraint.

Then it was he who bent over her. It was she who closed her eyes and gasped at the touch of his mouth and hands and moaned softly in supplication, and became frenzied in request until he took her in a triumphant joining that brought cries from both of them. The first time it was a wild, soaring, uncontrollable clashing and taking that ended in an ecstasy which was almost agony for both of them.

They rested. They talked softly, and after a while they again made love, happily and with deliberate easiness. Then they slept soundly for an hour.

When he awoke he stared at the ceiling in thought. He felt refreshed and relaxed. His mind was clear. The depressing cloud of frustration that had hung over him was gone.

Beside him, Lorrie stirred and spoke. "Awake?" she asked.

"Yes. Thinking. I've an idea about tomorrow. A good one."

She laughed a little. "Maybe there's something in what they say about needing, darling!"

"I know what I'm going to pitch," he said briskly. "Up, my love! We're going to the office. I'll call Helen and have her meet us there with one of the girls. We'll try to find Bill. Most of all I'll need you to rearrange our exhibits and stuff. Believe me, darling, we're going to make a pitch!"

CHAPTER ELEVEN

TWO HOURS BEFORE the presentation, Murch and Bill reviewed the last segment of the new presentation. Lorrie once again checked art work, layouts and graphs. Finally they were finished and sat down to relax, sleepy-eyed, drawn and tired.

Bill had joined Murch and Lorrie shortly after ten o'clock when they finally had reached him at his apartment. Helen and one girl had come to the office. It had been a long, grueling night.

Murch sighed. "We're as near set as we'll ever be. Lorrie, can't you go down to a beauty salon and get a facial or whatever a girl needs to revive her after a work session like that?"

"I'm going home for a shower and a change of clothing. And you'd better shave, both of you. You need clean shirts, too."

Bill stretched and yawned. "There's a barber and steam bath place on Fourth. How about it, Murch?"

"I have to make certain everything gets over there for the presentation. I'd better not—"

Helen said, "I've already ordered two taxis. I'll take care of all that."

Murch nodded. "It's a deal. And I want you there, Helen."

"I'll be there," she assured him.

They sent Lorrie home in a taxi, telling the driver to wait until she was ready to return.

"Meet us at LeLane's," he told her.

"I'll be there on time," she promised. Murch gave the driver a ten-dollar bill. "Stay out of accidents," he warned. "You have valuable cargo!"

Murch and Bill bought fresh shirts. They took almost an hour for shaves and steaming, followed by rubdowns and cold showers. When they came out they felt like different men.

They found a taxi and gave LeLane's address. As they sat back in the taxi, Bill said, "I was out with Kate last night."

"I don't know if you sound ominous or pleased," Murch said.

"Just making conversation," Bill hedged. "She pitched this morning. I wonder what they thought."

"We'll know later," Murch said.

They were early. They went immediately to the small auditorium that LeLane's used for sales meetings, fashion shows, and company gatherings. Lorrie and Helen were there.

The two men found most of their material in place on the small stage. A projection screen had been lowered, and a young man from LeLane's staff was following suggestions and directions from Lorrie and Helen.

Lorrie wore a smart summer ensemble that looked suspiciously like something from LeLane's line, and no one could have worn it to better advantage. The two women greeted the men.

"Shaves and clean shirts are an improvement," Helen Vaughan said. "We're almost ready. Isn't Lorrie beautiful in that ensemble? LeLane's, of course!"

The young man from the LeLane's staff grinned. He glanced at a wrist watch. "Any moment now," he said. "There'll be about thirty. Good luck!"

They thanked him and watched him leave. For a moment there was an awkward moment of silence among the four.

Helen said, "Do you want me to stay in here?"

"Of course!" Murch told her. He went on the stage to a speaker's stand. His script was there. He nervously flipped a switch by a microphone and tried his voice. He looked a question at the others.

"Okay," Bill said.

Suddenly Murch swore softly. "Who's going to run that damned projection machine? We should have hired an operator."

Maggie's up there," Helen assured him, glancing at the projection booth.

"Our Maggie? The stenographer?"

"Why not?" Helen said. "She takes and prints pictures—and wins prizes with them. And she has a better projection machine than they have. She's up there waiting."

Murch laughed in relief and looked at the booth. Maggie's freckled young face smiled down at him through an opening.

"Well, thank God for Maggie!" Murch called out, and it broke the tension in the room.

The door at the back opened and Sam Gortzein came in, followed by Pete Lanham, other department heads, and a retinue of underlings.

Gortzein walked to the stage and shook hands with Murch. He looked over the audience that was finding seats. When they were settled, the thin, dried old man held up a hand.

"All right," he said. "This is Murch Colton. So if there is nothing else, we give him the spotlight!" He smiled at Murch, shook hands with him again, and left the stage.

Momentarily Murch felt the familiar tight feeling of stage fright that he usually felt just before a presentation. Words deserted him. The presentation was a blank. He felt lost.

He took a deep breath and smiled. The fright would leave him as soon as he spoke. It always did. He went to the stand

and snapped the switch. He leaned forward slightly toward the microphone.

"It is just possible," he said, "that for the last few years a great many of us advertising people have been the biggest damned fools in the world! I'm just about to prove that! And when I'm finished, your firm and mine will know how to make more sales and greater profits than we have ever made!"

He stopped to smile. The fear was completely gone. The excitement of his own presentation was upon him now. Confidence and enthusiasm were crisp in his voice. He saw his audience smile and lean forward a little. He remembered Bill's trusted AIDA. *Attention.* He had it. They were hooked. And now straight down the line!

"I don't doubt," he continued, "that in previous presentations fine advertising campaigns have been roughed out for you.

"I am certain that you have had sound media-buying programs offered. You have been told what you should pay to obtain so many impacts.

"You have heard figures, facts, theories. We, too, have figures, facts, and theories.

"This is typical of advertising. Part of the business. But I am going to talk more specifically about *your customers*—and the people *whom you want for customers!* Who they are. Where they are. And how to get them!

"This is not the usual market research presentation. This is a brand new concept; not only of *your* advertising effort, but of the way America lives today!"

He looked up at the projection booth.

"Maggie," he said. "Let's show them!"

She had discovered how to fade the lights, and now she did. Suddenly the projection screen on the stage was filled with what appeared to be a simplified road map of the United States.

"Obviously, the United States," Murch said. "And you see lines that appear to be highways. They are. Highways of cities!"

The slide changed. The highways were blocked out in broad segments, each lettered. Murch said, "What you see are actually cities built along major highways—frequently freeways. Out here in the West, the one you see that runs from Los Angeles up to San Francisco is typical—actually one, long, heavily populated city—the megalopolis—one town merging into another.

"We have thirteen of these sprawling strip cities—interurbia.

"They're vitally important to *you* because *almost one-half of our purchasing citizens live in these strip cities!*"

He signaled Maggie. A new slide appeared on the screen. He allowed time for the figures to sink in.

Boston to Washington Approx.	31,500,000 persons
Albany to Erie	3,500,000
Cleveland to Pittsburgh	6,500,000
Detroit to Muskegon	5,750,000
Chicago to Milwaukee	8,500,000
Kansas City to Sioux Falls	2,100,000
St. Louis to Peoria	2,750,000
Toledo to Cincinnati	2,660,000
Atlanta to Raleigh	2,200,000
Miami-Tampa-Jacksonville	3,000,000
Fort Worth-Dallas-San Antonio-Houston	4,500,000
San Francisco to San Diego	13,600,000
Seattle to Eugene	2,500,000

He paused. A picture of a suburban city bordering a freeway flashed upon the screen.

"The fastest-buying, best-spending half of our population is concentrated in strip cities! They spend almost one hundred and ten billion dollars a year—about fifty-five per cent of the U. S. total."

On the screen flashed: $110,000,000,000! That was followed immediately by a picture of a housewife carrying packages.

Murch said, "Yesterday's housewife shopped two blocks from home. Today she shops two, twenty, fifty miles from home. Expressways, freeways, superhighways make it as easy to shop a city fifty miles away as to take a bus downtown."

Maggie changed the scene to a modern shopping center.

"And the super-shopping center," Murch said. "The mammoth supermarket. Already the corner drugstore apprehensively eyes the supermarket where proprietory drugs are racked near groceries. Already you can buy anything from a bikini to a pre-fabricated chicken-house under the same roof. And already—as you well know—*you're selling LeLane's products in huge shopping centers!*"

Murch looked out over his audience. Deliberately he said: "Do you think advertising methods designed and scaled to the old individual city, town or community works efficiently in this high-speed community economy? Certainly not!" He signaled for lights. They came up.

"In a few moments," he continued, "we'll show you how a modern, progressive agency employs new techniques to capture this market. But first, I want to discuss an important, specific group of buyers."

Again the lights went down. A picture of teen-agers at a football game filled the screen.

"Look at them!" Murch said. "Teen-agers of America! Eighteen million girls and boys between twelve and eighteen years of age. *They spend ten billion dollars a year!* They own more than eight hundred thousand cars! Three out of four own watches. Eight of ten have radios, and half of them own record players."

Murch paused. The picture changed to a group of high-school girls, all wearing LeLane's ensembles—a slide he had salvaged from the previous pitch.

"Remember," Murch said, "they know what they want to wear! And they *get* what they want! *I* want to see them wear LeLane's!"

On the screen appeared: A $10,000,000,000 market.

"Finally," Murch said, "a reminder that advertising directed at the one-half of a population that does *not* live in strip cities also calls for new methods. We intend to show you some!

"We have suggested advertising campaigns to cover both fields: specific media suggestions, budgets, new uses of radio and, most of all, television—which previously has not been too successful in the garment field, but soon will be with the advent of mass color television that can show our colors, fabrics, and unsurpassed styling to greater advantage.

"Above all, we bring you a new concept in advertising, precisely matched and mated to the new pattern of life in America!

"And now, before getting into specifics, I'm going to ask our Lorrie McPherson to show you her exciting fashion ads, conceived for LeLane's—new, fresh, vibrant; all the adjectives we like!"

Lorrie came to the stage with assurance. "We'll begin," she said, "with what we call the LeLane's *image*, a national campaign with ads your salesmen can carry in their portfolios to show the store buyers and say: "You can't afford *not* to carry our line when we pre-sell it for you with ads like these in *Vogue, Harper's Bazaar, McCall's, Mademoiselle.*"

There was a ripple of appreciative chuckles through the room. They knew this technique used by most fashion houses.

The lights went down. Suddenly a full-color reproduction of one of Lorrie's beautifully executed fashion ads filled the screen. After seconds of silence, a spontaneous wave of enthusiastic applause erupted.

Murch stopped holding his breath. This kind of applause from the toughened audience was the highest praise for Lorrie. They exchanged glances in the semidarkness, and he saw her lift her head and smile with complete confidence.

She signaled, and the slides began to appear in their scheduled order. Her commentary was terse and colorful. The enthusiasm was sustained, and even mounted. She had her audience.

She finished and Murch took the rostrum again. The audience stayed with him. Graphically, with the aid of slides, flipboard and blackboard, he outlined tentative ad campaigns, budgets, new techniques of marketing.

He made suggestions for promotions in the huge market centers. He described traveling fashion shows to appear in them. He outlined a plan for LeLane's clubs in high schools.

He demonstrated sales promotions that would encompass strip cities with saturation radio, television, shopping papers, city newspapers, and tie-ins with manufacturers of products outside the garment field.

Finally he explained his service-fee ideas, suggesting the possibilities.

He finished. The pitch was ended. He felt completely exhausted.

Bill grinned at him. Lorrie looked happy.

There was a gathering in front of the stage; LeLane's people trying to be casual and noncommittal. Murch looked at Sam Gortzein. The old man nodded.

"Your home is in the book?" he asked. "I'll let you know about eight."

Pete Lanham stood beside them. A faint mocking smile was on his lips when he spoke. "This wasn't the original pitch, of course, Mr. Gortzein," he said. "I just want to make certain you know that. All this stuff about strip cities and teen-agers— this comes from Murch. We had a completely different idea, McPherson and I. Frankly, I don't know what happened. What did happen, Murch?"

Murch smiled blandly. "Nothing, Pete. It's just a new agency now. They have you, CWC has Linda, and we have us. So we decided to be ourselves."

"We don't think you—" Pete started to say.

"Pete," Sam Gortzein interrupted softly. "*I* still do the thinking? Not *we*? No?" He looked innocently at his new employee.

The small man stared at the wizened old man through his black-rimmed glasses. Suddenly he blushed furiously.

"Yes, sir," he said. "Yes, Mr. Gortzein." He turned and hurriedly walked away. Murch and Gortzein watched him leave, and then looked at one another. The old man shrugged.

"A *schlemiel*?" he asked. "Or maybe he's forgetting who Sam Gortzein is?" He smiled at Murch as if he had made a great joke, and then turned and cheerfully followed his employees through the auditorium doorway.

CHAPTER TWELVE

T HIS WAS the waiting period.

Murch took them to dinner and afterwards invited them to his home. "Gortzein will call me there," he told them.

How simple it will be, he thought. *The telephone will ring. I'll answer. And a voice will tell me in a few words if we succeeded or failed.*

They drove to the house in Murch's car. He found a bottle of Scotch and Bill helped him fix drinks for the five of them: Lorrie, Helen, Maggie, Bill and Murch.

In the kitchen Murch said to Bill, "Have you called Kate?"

Bill shook his head. "Waiting," he said. "I think it's between Kate and us."

"I'm certain," Murch said. "And we're way out on a limb, Bill. We didn't go by the book. The strip city and teen-ager angles—some of the other ideas."

"I watched Gortzein. He was interested. So were the others. You had something they liked, Murch—enthusiasm. You were running over with it, and enthusiasm engenders enthusiasm."

"Pete?"

"To hell with him." Bill picked up a tray of drinks and headed for the living room. "Who needs him?"

Eight o'clock came and passed without a call. The waiting became almost agony. Did the delay mean good news or bad news? What was happening? Why didn't someone call?

At exactly thirteen minutes after eight the phone rang. Murch deliberately let it ring twice before he picked it up.

"Murch Colton speaking," he said.

Sam Gortzein's rasping voice came across the wires.

"This call I like to make," he said. "The others—no. Congratulations—you now are LeLane's advertising agency!"

Murch found himself holding his breath. He let it out silently and said, "Mr. Gortzein, we'll do a fine job for you. And thank you."

He glanced at the others and saw their delighted smiles. He confirmed their unasked question with an affirmative nod. Gortzein still was talking:

"But you should know, Murch, that it was close. I'm sorry we don't get Kate Rhodes or Linda Smith—most of all Kate Rhodes because she is a woman with all it takes in this business. But we like your Lorrie McPherson and your Bill Rhodes, even if he's a *schmo* to get divorced from a smart woman like Kate.

"Maybe you could talk business with her? She should join your firm maybe? And Murch—you make good sense with your strip-city business and what a market are teenagers, your traveling fashion shows, and what you call new techniques. They all add up that we give you a try. One year. And if that *goniff* Pete Lanham gives you trouble, let me know.

"I can use him for what he is, and you know what he is, and sometimes that I can use in the garment business. But when I spend like hundreds of thousands of dollars for advertising, Sam Gortzein does the deciding. This you should remember, Murch?"

"This I already know," Murch said with a smile.

"Okay. Tell the little girl who operated the picture machine that she did good, too!" The telephone clicked in Murch's ear.

Murch looked into the waiting, eager faces. No one seemed to know exactly what to say. Then Murch laughed.

"We did it!" he announced. "We're in!"

Almost immediately the telephone began to ring. The president of the other local competing agency called with congratulations. Pete Lanham called and tried to sound happy for them. The third call was from Kate Rhodes.

"Murch, I'm thrilled for you! I hear you were terrific! Sam Gortzein admitted it."

"We barely nosed you out, Kate. You know that, too."

"I tried," she said lightly. "Is Bill there?"

"Certainly." Murch handed the telephone to Bill and went to get a drink. When he returned, Bill looked at him over the telephone mouthpiece.

"Murch, I couldn't tell you before, but Kate and I have a reconciliation cooking on the front burner, and she's another nice dish on a back burner. She wants to know if she can buy in with me? Could you stand a husband-wife team of Rhodes?"

Murch stared at him in amazement, and finally took the telephone from Bill's hand and said into it: "Kate—you just married a whole damned agency!"

He heard her laugh happily as he returned the telephone to Bill.

"Kate," Bill said, "I didn't ask you—where are you? I mean, we're celebrating and—"

"Where *am* I?" she asked, as if shocked. "In my hotel room! I just got into something comfortable—wholly inadequate for anything three feet away from a bedroom, but terribly adequate for what I have in mind. I'm waiting."

"I can't think of a better thing to do!" he said. "Stay right there!"

He had been gone less than half an hour, and Helen and Maggie had just departed in a taxi, when the telephone drew

Murch away from Lorrie where they stood at a window looking at the view and talking.

He answered the call and Diana said, "Murch? I just wondered how you came out with the presentation."

"We got the account."

"How wonderful! Congratulations! Murch, about Rick Andes. I didn't want to call before. I was afraid you'd blame me. But that's all over. I mean between Rick and me. And I thought—"

Murch grasped the telephone tightly and looked to the outlined figure of Lorrie where she stood at the window. He sensed what Diana was trying to do. She had split with Rick Andes and now she was sounding out the climate she had deserted.

"No, Diana," he said quietly. "Don't even try. There's nothing left for us. What did remain died unpleasantly one morning at the beach. You didn't wake up to watch it die. Remember?"

"I suppose you and that slut Lorrie McPherson haven't been—"

"Stop it," he said curtly. "You asked for a divorce. You'll have it."

"And at a price!" she said angrily. "I mean it, Murch. I want everything I can get. And you can't afford a scandal. Sam Gortzein is touchy about things like that."

Murch fought his own anger again. *Whatever the cost might be*, he thought, *it's worth it!*

"Have your lawyer call me," he said. He dropped the telephone in its cradle.

Lorrie came to him. "Diana?" she asked.

He nodded. "I imagine you heard enough to know."

"I know that I love you," she said. She stood on her toes and kissed him firmly on the mouth. She stepped back quickly. "Take me home, Murch. I don't want to stay here any longer tonight. Her call is still in the room. I only want to think about *us* tonight."

They drove the few blocks to her home. There was a letter in the mailbox from Mike. She read it quickly.

"He says he's going to Reno with Laddie. He'll get the divorce, if that's all right with me." She shook her head. "Usually it's the woman, isn't it, Murch?"

"Yes. He's sick, Lorrie."

"And I can't cure him."

They went into the study and she turned on a light and went to an easel. She picked up her picture of the Negro girl that he had admired only a relatively few nights before.

"Remember?" she asked.

"You said, quote: ' ... *she's not for sale. She's too much a part of me, and I never sell any of me.*' "

Lorrie smiled again, happy that he remembered. She picked up the picture and looked at it, finally nodding in satisfaction.

She said, "And then I told you, quote: '*I never sell any of me. I only give.*' "

She held out the picture to him. "Here, Murch. It's yours—all my gifts are now for you."

"It's beautiful—pagan, lovely, beautiful ... a woman." He took the picture and they left the study.

Without speaking they went to the guest room that they already knew. Then there was a moment when she stood not far from the picture where he had placed it against a wall. In that moment he looked at the picture and saw the nubile splendor of the Negro girl in her primitive, earthy beauty. Then his eyes sought the contrasting loveliness that was Lorrie's as she stood tall and nude and waiting for his eyes and touch.

"I wonder," he said, "how far we've really come, or if man has ever dreamed a finer dream, or sought a better reward than this. Wars have been fought, empires built, fortunes earned, books written, pictures painted, music composed—yet when men have finished and look back, I wonder if the most secret, finest memories are not those single, short, wonderful hours when a man and a woman are together. I wonder ..."

She smiled and said, "Men and words." She came to him and he embraced her. They kissed, deep and long.

"I'm out of words," he murmured. "I used them all today."

"You don't need words for the rest of it," she whispered. "Not a single one ..."

The End